William Shakespeare's
Romeo and Juliet
In Plain and Simple English

BookCaps
www.bookcaps.com

D0514616

Prologue

Chorus	**Chorus**
Two families with similar social standing, Located in Verona, Italy, Hold an old grudge which develops into a new controversy, Where seemingly civilized people commit murder.	Two households, both alike in dignity, In fair Verona, where we lay our scene, From ancient grudge break to new mutiny, Where civil blood makes civil hands unclean. From forth the fatal loins of these two foes
Two children of the warring families, Fall in love and take their lives, And in the process destroy, Their parents' will to fight.	A pair of star-cross'd lovers take their life; Whose misadventur'd piteous overthrows Doth with their death bury their parents' strife.
The events leading up to the young deaths, And the mutual hatred held by their parents, Which could only be softened by their children's suicide, Is the subject of the play.	The fearful passage of their death-mark'd love, And the continuance of their parents' rage, Which but their children's end naught could remove, Is now the two hours' traffic of our stage;
If you watch and listen patiently, What is missing from this prologue will be shown on stage.	The which, if you with patient ears attend, What here shall miss, our toil shall strive to mend.

Act 1

Scene 1

A public place	**A public place.**
(Enter Sampson and Gregory, armed with swords and bucklers, or shields.)	(Enter Sampson and Gregory armed with swords and bucklers.)

Sampson

I swear, Gregory, we will not stand by and be treated like servants.

Gregory

We are servants, fool.

Sampson

I mean, if they want to fight, I'm ready.

Gregory

The only thing you will fight is the death penalty.

Sampson

I will fight in a minute, if someone messes with me.

Gregory

Well then, no one has messed with you in a long time, huh?

Sampson

A Montague can make me angry enough to fight!

Gregory

To be angry is to react and to be brave is to stand and fight; therefore, your reaction has always been to run.

Sampson

I will never run away from a Montague: I will take him down, and if he is not careful, his wife, too.

Gregory

That shows what an idiot you are, to prey on the weakest of the Montagues.

Sampson

Gregory, o' my word, we'll not carry coals.

Gregory

No, for then we should be colliers.

Sampson

I mean, an we be in choler we'll draw.

Gregory

Ay, while you live, draw your neck out o' the collar.

Sampson

I strike quickly, being moved.

Gregory

But thou art not quickly moved to strike.

Sampson

A dog of the house of Montague moves me.

Gregory

To move is to stir; and to be valiant is to stand: therefore, if thou art moved, thou runn'st away.

Sampson

A dog of that house shall move me to stand: I will take the wall of any man or maid of Montague's.

Gregory

That shows thee a weak slave; for the weakest goes to the wall.

Sampson
I will push the Montagues into a fight and make their women watch.

Gregory
This is not our fight! This war is between our masters.

Sampson
It's all for one and one for all. I will kill all of the Montagues, both women and men.

Gregory
Why the women?

Sampson
Well, maybe not kill them; only make them wish they were dead. If you know what I mean?

Gregory
Yes, I know what you mean. But I doubt the women will.

Sampson
Oh, they'll know what I mean, when I stand over them with my "weapon" exposed.

Gregory
(Referring to Sampson's genitals.) More like, you standing over them with a limp noodle. Draw your weapon, two from the house of Montague approach.

Sampson
I have my sword. Start an argument and I'll back you up.

Gregory
How will you back me up? Turn your back on

Sampson
True; and therefore women, being the weaker vessels, are ever thrust to the wall: therefore I will push Montague's men from the wall and thrust his maids to the wall.

Gregory
The quarrel is between our masters and us their men.

Sampson
Tis all one, I will show myself a tyrant: when I have fought with the men I will be cruel with the maids, I will cut off their heads.

Gregory. The heads of the maids?

Sampso
Ay, the heads of the maids, or their maidenheads; take it in what sense thou wilt.

Gregory
They must take it in sense that feel it.

Sampson
Me they shall feel while I am able to stand: and 'tis known I am a pretty piece of flesh.

Gregory
'Tis well thou art not fish; if thou hadst, thou hadst been poor-John.--Draw thy tool; Here comes two of the house of Montagues.

Sampson
My naked weapon is out: quarrel! I will back thee.

Gregory
How! turn thy back and run?

me and run?

Sampson
Quit worrying.

Gregory
No, you wimp. I will fear fighting with you as my partner.

Sampson
Fine then. Let's be law-abiding citizens. Let them pass and see if they will start with us.

Gregory
I will stare them down as they pass by, and let them take it as they wish.

Sampson
You mean, as they dare. I will flip them off and see what they do. If they ignore me, we know they are cowards.

(Enter Abraham and Balthasar.)

Abraham
Did you just flip me off?

Sampson
Uhhh…I did point my middle finger skyward.

Abraham
I said, "Did YOU just flip me off?"

Sampson
(To Gregory) Am I still abiding the law, if I say yes?

Gregory
I don't think so.

Sampson
No sir, I was just pointing my middle finger towards the sky.

Sampson
Fear me not.

Gregory
No, marry; I fear thee!

Sampson
Let us take the law of our sides; let them begin.

Gregory
I will frown as I pass by; and let them take it as they list.

Sampson
Nay, as they dare. I will bite my thumb at them; which is disgrace to them if they bear it.

[Enter Abraham and Balthasar.]

Abraham
Do you bite your thumb at us, sir?

Sampson
I do bite my thumb, sir.

Abraham
Do you bite your thumb at us, sir?

Sampson
Is the law of our side if I say ay?

Gregory
No.

Sampson
No, sir, I do not bite my thumb at you, sir; but I bite my thumb, sir.

Gregory Are you trying to start a fight, sir?	**Gregory** Do you quarrel, sir?
Abraham A fight, sir? No sir!	**Abraham** Quarrel, sir! no, sir.
Sampson Well, if you want a fight. I am your man. My master is just as good as yours.	**Sampson** But if you do, sir, am for you: I serve as good a man as you.
Abraham But, not better than mine.	**Abraham** No better.
Sampson Well…	**Sampson** Well, sir.
Gregory Say yes. Here comes one of our master's relatives.	**Gregory** Say better; here comes one of my master's kinsmen.
Sampson Yes, Mr. Montague is better than your master.	**Sampson** Yes, better, sir.
Abraham Liar!	**Abraham** You lie.
Sampson Then we will fight! Remember Gregory, you are a better fighter than me.	**Sampson** Draw, if you be men.--Gregory, remember thy swashing blow.
(They fight.)	[They fight.]
(Enter Benvolio.)	[Enter Benvolio.]
Benvolio What is going on here? Put away your weapons, fools. You don't know what you are doing.	**Benvolio** Part, fools! put up your swords; you know not what you do.
(Beats down their weapons with his sword.)	[Beats down their swords.]
(Enter Tybalt.)	[Enter Tybalt.]
Tybalt	**Tybalt**

Are you using your sword against these weak men? Turn around, Benvolio, and use it against someone as strong as you, if you dare.

Benvolio
I am only trying to break up their fight. So, put up your sword or use it to help me.

Tybalt
Right, you expect me to believe you, a peacekeeper? I hate the word, peace, as I hate hell, all Montagues, and YOU. Fight, you coward!

(They fight.)

(Enter several members of both families, who join in. Then, enter Citizens with clubs.)

Citizens
Everyone, draw your clubs, swords, spears.
Beat them down.
Down with the Capulets.
Down with the Montagues.

(Enter Capulet in his gown, with Lady Capulet.)

Capulet
What is going on here? Someone hand me my sword.

Lady Capulet
A weapon, a weapon? Why do you need your sword?

Capulet
Give me my sword. Here comes Old Montague with a weapon drawn.

(Enter Montague with Lady Montague.)

Montague
My enemy, Capulet! Let me at him. Don't hold me back.

What, art thou drawn among these heartless hinds? Turn thee Benvolio, look upon thy death.

Benvolio
I do but keep the peace: put up thy sword, Or manage it to part these men with me.

Tybalt
What, drawn, and talk of peace! I hate the word As I hate hell, all Montagues, and thee: Have at thee, coward!

[They fight.]

[Enter several of both Houses, who join the fray; then enter Citizens with clubs.]

1 Citizen
Clubs, bills, and partisans! strike! beat them down! Down with the Capulets! Down with the Montagues!

[Enter Capulet in his gown, and Lady Capulet.]

Capulet
What noise is this?--Give me my long sword, ho!

Lady Capulet
A crutch, a crutch!--Why call you for a sword?

Capulet
My sword, I say!--Old Montague is come, And flourishes his blade in spite of me.

[Enter Montague and his Lady Montague.]

Montague
Thou villain Capulet!-- Hold me not, let me go.

Lady Montague
You are not going anywhere. (Holding onto Montague.)

(Enter the Prince and his Attendants.)

Prince
Stop you criminals, enemies of peace, cowards who use weapons to settle your disputes and beasts who seek the blood of your enemies to solve your problems. I'll have you arrested and punished, if you don't listen to me. Put down you weapons and listen. Three times, you have fought over senseless words. You, Capulet, and you, Montague, have disturbed the peace three times. And, the Citizens of Verona have had to stop you. If you ever fight again, you will pay with your lives. Everyone go back to your businesses or go home. Capulet, you come with me. And, Montague, you come this afternoon. I am going to get to the bottom of this feud. This is your last chance. Now go!

(Exit Prince, Attendants, Capulet, Lady Capulet, Tybalt, Citizens, and Servants.)

Montague
Who started this fight? Did you see what happened, Benvolio?

Benvolio
All I saw was your servants fighting two of the Capulet servants. I tried to break them apart and that arrogant Tybalt showed up. He was getting ready to kill me. He took a swing at me with his sword, but missed. I wasn't about to

Lady Montague
Thou shalt not stir one foot to seek a foe.

[Enter Prince, with Attendants.]

Prince
Rebellious subjects, enemies to peace, Profaners of this neighbour-stained steel,-- Will they not hear?--What, ho! you men, you beasts, That quench the fire of your pernicious rage With purple fountains issuing from your veins,-- On pain of torture, from those bloody hands Throw your mistemper'd weapons to the ground And hear the sentence of your moved prince.-- Three civil brawls, bred of an airy word, By thee, old Capulet, and Montague, Have thrice disturb'd the quiet of our streets; And made Verona's ancient citizens Cast by their grave beseeming ornaments, To wield old partisans, in hands as old, Canker'd with peace, to part your canker'd hate: If ever you disturb our streets again, Your lives shall pay the forfeit of the peace. For this time, all the rest depart away:-- You, Capulet, shall go along with me;-- And, Montague, come you this afternoon, To know our farther pleasure in this case, To old Free-town, our common judgment-place.-- Once more, on pain of death, all men depart.

[Exeunt Prince and Attendants; Capulet, Lady Capulet, Tybalt, Citizens, and Servants.]

Montague
Who set this ancient quarrel new abroach?-- Speak, nephew, were you by when it began?

Benvolio
Here were the servants of your adversary And yours, close fighting ere I did approach: I drew to part them: in the instant came The fiery Tybalt, with his sword prepar'd; Which, as he breath'd defiance to my ears, He swung about

stand there and be killed, so I defended myself. Then, the prince showed up and broke us apart.

Lady Montague
Oh, where is Romeo? Have you seen him today? I am so glad he was not there.

Benvolio
I saw him early this morning while on a walk to clear my head. He was underneath the grove of sycamore trees, growing on the west side of the city. When he saw me, he took off into the woods. I didn't go after him, because I thought he must have wanted to be alone.

Montague
He has been seen many times in that place, crying and depressed. As soon as he gets home, he locks himself up in his bedroom, where he draws the curtains and stays in the dark. He must be in a bad mood and need counseling.

Benvolio
Do you know why he is depressed?

Montague
I don't know, nor do I know how to go about finding the reason for his depression.

his head, and cut the winds, Who, nothing hurt withal, hiss'd him in scorn: While we were interchanging thrusts and blows, Came more and more, and fought on part and part, Till the prince came, who parted either part.

Lady Montague
O, where is Romeo?--saw you him to-day?-- Right glad I am he was not at this fray.

Benvolio
Madam, an hour before the worshipp'd sun Peer'd forth the golden window of the east, A troubled mind drave me to walk abroad; Where,--underneath the grove of sycamore That westward rooteth from the city's side,-- So early walking did I see your son: Towards him I made; but he was ware of me, And stole into the covert of the wood: I, measuring his affections by my own,-- That most are busied when they're most alone,-- Pursu'd my humour, not pursuing his, And gladly shunn'd who gladly fled from me.

Montague
Many a morning hath he there been seen, With tears augmenting the fresh morning's dew, Adding to clouds more clouds with his deep sighs: But all so soon as the all-cheering sun Should in the farthest east begin to draw The shady curtains from Aurora's bed, Away from light steals home my heavy son, And private in his chamber pens himself; Shuts up his windows, locks fair daylight out And makes himself an artificial night: Black and portentous must this humour prove, Unless good counsel may the cause remove.

Benvolio
My noble uncle, do you know the cause?

Montague
I neither know it nor can learn of him.

Benvolio
Have you tried to make him tell you?

Montague
I have, and many of our friends have tried. He stays to himself and keeps his secrets close. It is like he is being eaten up inside. We would do anything to help him, if we only knew what was wrong.

Benvolio
Here he comes, so let me try.

Montague
I would be more than happy for you to.

(Exit Montague with Lady Montague.)

(Enter Romeo)

Benvolio
Good morning, cousin.

Romeo
Is it morning?

Benvolio
It is only 9 o'clock.

Romeo
My sadness does not know time. Was that my father leaving so fast?

Benvolio
Yes, it was. What makes you so sad that time stands still.

Benvolio
Have you importun'd him by any means?

Montague
Both by myself and many other friends; But he, his own affections' counsellor, Is to himself,--I will not say how true,-- But to himself so secret and so close, So far from sounding and discovery, As is the bud bit with an envious worm Ere he can spread his sweet leaves to the air, Or dedicate his beauty to the sun. Could we but learn from whence his sorrows grow, We would as willingly give cure as know.

Benvolio
See, where he comes: so please you step aside; I'll know his grievance or be much denied.

Montague
I would thou wert so happy by thy stay To hear true shrift.--Come, madam, let's away,

[Exeunt Montague and Lady.]

[Enter Romeo.]

Benvolio
Good morrow, cousin.

Romeo
Is the day so young?

Benvolio
But new struck nine.

Romeo
Ay me! sad hours seem long. Was that my father that went hence so fast?

Benvolio
It was.--What sadness lengthens Romeo's hours?

Romeo
Wanting what I cannot have.

Benvolio
Are you in love?

Romeo
Out…

Benvolio
Out of love?

Romeo
No, she is out of love with me.

Benvolio
Love looks nice from the outside but can be very painful inside.

Romeo
Love is blind. Ha! Love will make you do whatever it wants; it controls you. Let's go eat. (Sees blood on Benvolio.) Oh, no! What happened? Don't tell me. I know all about it, the trouble of those who love to hate, and hateful love. Sickening beauty, feather of lead, bright darkness, cold fire, sick health! That is what love is, confusing and contradictory. This is the love I feel. Are you laughing at me?

Benvolio
No, I would rather cry than laugh at you.

Romeo
Cry, at what?

Benvolio
At your foul disposition.

Romeo
Not having that which, having, makes them short.

Benvolio
In love?

Romeo
Out,--

Benvolio
Of love?

Romeo
Out of her favour where I am in love.

Benvolio
Alas, that love, so gentle in his view, Should be so tyrannous and rough in proof!

Romeo
Alas that love, whose view is muffled still, Should, without eyes, see pathways to his will!-- Where shall we dine?--O me!--What fray was here? Yet tell me not, for I have heard it all. Here's much to do with hate, but more with love:-- Why, then, O brawling love! O loving hate! O anything, of nothing first create! O heavy lightness! serious vanity! Mis-shapen chaos of well-seeming forms! Feather of lead, bright smoke, cold fire, sick health! Still-waking sleep, that is not what it is!-- This love feel I, that feel no love in this. Dost thou not laugh?

Benvolio
No, coz, I rather weep.

Romeo
Good heart, at what?

Benvolio
At thy good heart's oppression.

Romeo
I feel so heavy at heart, and yet, you want to add your sadness to mine. I cannot take anymore. Love is a smoldering fire ignited by your lover's eyes. Love is an ocean created by your lover's tears. It is a secret madness, a poison, a savory sweet. I am out of here. Goodbye, Benvolio.

(Going)

Benvolio
Hey, you can't leave me like this. I will go with you.

Romeo
With me? You don't know me. I am not Romeo. I do not even know who I am anymore.

Benvolio
Tell me who it is you love?

Romeo
Why? What good will it do?

Benvolio
It will make you feel better to tell someone.

Romeo
Leave me alone and just let me be sad. All I can say is that I am in love with a woman.

Benvolio
I knew that much.

Romeo
Well, good job. She is a beautiful woman.

Benvolio

Romeo
Why, such is love's transgression.-- Griefs of mine own lie heavy in my breast; Which thou wilt propagate, to have it prest With more of thine: this love that thou hast shown Doth add more grief to too much of mine own. Love is a smoke rais'd with the fume of sighs; Being purg'd, a fire sparkling in lovers' eyes; Being vex'd, a sea nourish'd with lovers' tears: What is it else? a madness most discreet, A choking gall, and a preserving sweet.-- Farewell, my coz.

[Going.]

Benvolio
Soft! I will go along: An if you leave me so, you do me wrong.

Romeo
Tut! I have lost myself; I am not here: This is not Romeo, he's some other where.

Benvolio
Tell me in sadness who is that you love?

Romeo
What, shall I groan and tell thee?

Benvolio
Groan! why, no; But sadly tell me who.

Romeo
Bid a sick man in sadness make his will,-- Ah, word ill urg'd to one that is so ill!-- In sadness, cousin, I do love a woman.

Benvolio. I aim'd so near when I suppos'd you lov'd.

Romeo
A right good markman!--And she's fair I love.

Benvolio

I figured that much. Cupid's arrow always hits the beautiful ones first.

Romeo
Well, you're wrong about that. She has not been pierced by Cupids arrow. She has the goddess, Diana's, wit, and she vows to remain chaste. She will not allow herself to fall in love or even be looked at as the object of love. She will not accept gifts and her beauty is going to die with her.

Benvolio
You mean, she has sworn to stay a virgin all of her life?

Romeo
She has and what a waste. Beauty like hers is rare, but it will end with her since she will not have children. Oh, how I want her, but cannot have her. I feel like I am going to die.

Benvolio
Listen to me. Stop thinking about her.

Romeo
I would if I could. Teach me how.

Benvolio
Listen to me. Look for someone else. There are many beautiful girls out there.

Romeo
What good would it do? Once you have seen the most beautiful girl, no other one will do. They pale in comparison. So leave me alone now. You cannot help me.

A right fair mark, fair coz, is soonest hit.

Romeo
Well, in that hit you miss: she'll not be hit With Cupid's arrow,--she hath Dian's wit; And, in strong proof of chastity well arm'd, From love's weak childish bow she lives unharm'd. She will not stay the siege of loving terms Nor bide th' encounter of assailing eyes, Nor ope her lap to saint-seducing gold: O, she's rich in beauty; only poor That, when she dies, with beauty dies her store.

Benvolio
Then she hath sworn that she will still live chaste?

Romeo
She hath, and in that sparing makes huge waste; For beauty, starv'd with her severity, Cuts beauty off from all posterity. She is too fair, too wise; wisely too fair, To merit bliss by making me despair: She hath forsworn to love; and in that vow Do I live dead that live to tell it now.

Benvolio
Be rul'd by me, forget to think of her.

Romeo
O, teach me how I should forget to think.

Benvolio
By giving liberty unto thine eyes; Examine other beauties.

Romeo
'Tis the way To call hers, exquisite, in question more: These happy masks that kiss fair ladies' brows, Being black, puts us in mind they hide the fair; He that is strucken blind cannot forget The precious treasure of his eyesight lost: Show me a mistress that is passing fair, What doth her beauty serve but as a note Where I may read

Benvolio
I will help you, or die trying.

(Exit all.)

who pass'd that passing fair? Farewell: thou
canst not teach me to forget.

Benvolio
I'll pay that doctrine, or else die in debt.

[Exeunt.]

Scene II: A Street

(Enter Capulet, Paris, and Servant.)

Capulet
If both Montague and I are alike and receive the same penalty, I do not think we will have a hard time keeping the peace.

Paris
True, you are both honorable men, and it is a shame that you have been at this feud for so long. So, what do you think about my proposition?

Capulet
My daughter is only thirteen years old. Let's wait a couple more years for her to mature, before we make her a bride.

Paris
Many girls younger than her are mothers by now.

Capulet
However, those girls marry too young. My daughter means the world to me. So, date her, Paris, and try to win her heart, because my consent means nothing, if she does not agree. Why don't you come to my house tonight? We are having a party and I have invited many of my friends. One more guest won't hurt. You will be surrounded by young girls, as many as the stars in the skies. After that, you may not have your heart set on my daughter. Here is a list of the guests. (Hands Servant a

Capulet
But Montague is bound as well as I, In penalty alike; and 'tis not hard, I think, For men so old as we to keep the peace.

Paris
Of honourable reckoning are you both; And pity 'tis you liv'd at odds so long. But now, my lord, what say you to my suit?

Capulet
But saying o'er what I have said before: My child is yet a stranger in the world, She hath not seen the change of fourteen years; Let two more summers wither in their pride Ere we may think her ripe to be a bride.

Paris
Younger than she are happy mothers made.

Capulet
And too soon marr'd are those so early made. The earth hath swallowed all my hopes but she,-- She is the hopeful lady of my earth: But woo her, gentle Paris, get her heart, My will to her consent is but a part; An she agree, within her scope of choice Lies my consent and fair according voice. This night I hold an old accustom'd feast, Whereto I have invited many a guest, Such as I love; and you among the store, One more, most welcome, makes my number more. At my poor house look

paper.) Go find the people on this list and tell them they are invited to the party. Come on, Paris. Let's go.

(Exit Capulet and Paris.)

Servant
Find the guests on the list! A shoemaker works in his yard, a tailor works on his art, a fisher works with his pencil and a painter works with his nets! Me, I am sent to find his guests whose names I cannot make out. I must learn to read, eventually! Here comes someone to help me.

(Enter Benvolio and Romeo.)

Benvolio
Hey, one man loses a lover while another one gains, and one man finds pain while another one's is taken away. Don't be so hard on yourself. Look up. If you find a new girl, you will feel better.

Romeo
You think you know the cure for what ails me.

to behold this night Earth-treading stars that make dark heaven light: Such comfort as do lusty young men feel When well apparell'd April on the heel Of limping winter treads, even such delight Among fresh female buds shall you this night Inherit at my house; hear all, all see, And like her most whose merit most shall be: Which, among view of many, mine, being one, May stand in number, though in reckoning none. Come, go with me.-- Go, sirrah, trudge about Through fair Verona; find those persons out Whose names are written there, [gives a paper] and to them say, My house and welcome on their pleasure stay.

[Exeunt Capulet and Paris].

Servant.
Find them out whose names are written here! It is written that the shoemaker should meddle with his yard and the tailor with his last, the fisher with his pencil, and the painter with his nets; but I am sent to find those persons whose names are here writ, and can never find what names the writing person hath here writ. I must to the learned:--in good time!

[Enter Benvolio and Romeo.]

Benvolio
Tut, man, one fire burns out another's burning, One pain is lessen'd by another's anguish; Turn giddy, and be holp by backward turning; One desperate grief cures with another's languish: Take thou some new infection to thy eye, And the rank poison of the old will die.

Romeo
Your plantain-leaf is excellent for that.

Benvolio
Cure for what?

Romeo
My broken leg.

Benvolio
Are you crazy, Romeo?

Romeo
Only crazy in love, crazy like a locked-up madman hungering for food and tortured every day. (To Servant) Hello.

Servant
Good evening, sir. May I ask if you can read?

Romeo
I can read my fortune and it is miserable.

Servant
Perhaps you have graduated from the school of hard knocks, but can you read words?

Romeo
If I know the language, I can read it.

Servant
Wise guy, eh? Well, have a good day.

Romeo
Stay, man. I'm just in a foul mood. I can read.
(Reads.) Sir Martino and his wife and daughters; Count Anselmo and his beautiful sisters; the widow of Vitruvio; Sir Placentio and his lovely nieces; Mercutio and his brother Valentine; mine uncle Capulet, his wife, and daughters; my fair niece Rosaline; Livia; Sir Valentio

Benvolio
For what, I pray thee?

Romeo
For your broken shin.

Benvolio
Why, Romeo, art thou mad?

Romeo
Not mad, but bound more than a madman is; Shut up in prison, kept without my food, Whipp'd and tormented and--God-den, good fellow.

Servant
God gi' go-den.--I pray, sir, can you read?

Romeo
Ay, mine own fortune in my misery.

Servant
Perhaps you have learned it without book: but I pray, can you read anything you see?

Romeo
Ay, If I know the letters and the language.

Servant
Ye say honestly: rest you merry!

Romeo
Stay, fellow; I can read. [Reads.] 'Signior Martino and his wife and daughters; County Anselmo and his beauteous sisters; the lady widow of Vitruvio; Signior Placentio and his lovely nieces; Mercutio and his brother Valentine; mine uncle Capulet, his wife, and daughters; my fair niece Rosaline; Livia; Signior Valentio and his cousin Tybalt; Lucio and

and his cousin Tybalt; Lucio and the lively Helena. A good list you have here. (Returns the paper.) For what is this list?

Servant
A party?

Romeo
Where?

Servant
A dinner party is being thrown at our house.

Romeo
Whose house?

Servant
My master's house.

Romeo
I should have asked who your master was in the first place.

Servant
I'll tell you. My master is the great and rich Capulet, and if you are not related to the Montagues, then come to the party. Good Evening!

(Exit Servant.)

Benvolio
Rosaline is going to be at the party with all of the other beautiful girls of Verona. Let's go and compare her to the others. I'll show you she is not as perfect as you think.

Romeo
Finding someone as beautiful as her is

the lively Helena.' A fair assembly. [Gives back the paper]: whither should they come?

Servant
Up.

Romeo
Whither?

Servant
To supper; to our house.

Romeo
Whose house?

Servant
My master's.

Romeo
Indeed I should have ask'd you that before.

Servant
Now I'll tell you without asking: my master is the great rich Capulet; and if you be not of the house of Montagues, I pray, come and crush a cup of wine. Rest you merry!

[Exit.]

Benvolio
At this same ancient feast of Capulet's Sups the fair Rosaline whom thou so lov'st; With all the admired beauties of Verona. Go thither; and, with unattainted eye, Compare her face with some that I shall show, And I will make thee think thy swan a crow.

Romeo
When the devout religion of mine eye

impossible. Even speaking of such a thing makes you a liar and makes me want to tear out my eyes. The sun has never set upon another as beautiful as Rosaline.

Benvolio
Well, it won't hurt to just look. If you don't see anyone as beautiful, fine, but if you do…

Romeo
Fine, I'll go with you, but only to see my love.

(Exit Benvolio and Romeo.)

Maintains such falsehood, then turn tears to fires; And these,--who, often drown'd, could never die,-- Transparent heretics, be burnt for liars! One fairer than my love? the all-seeing sun Ne'er saw her match since first the world begun.

Benvolio
Tut, you saw her fair, none else being by, Herself pois'd with herself in either eye: But in that crystal scales let there be weigh'd Your lady's love against some other maid That I will show you shining at this feast, And she shall scant show well that now shows best.

Romeo
I'll go along, no such sight to be shown, But to rejoice in splendour of my own.

[Exeunt.]

Scene III: Room in Capulet's House

(Enter Lady Capulet and nurse.)

Lady Capulet
Nurse, where's my daughter? Bring her to me.

Nurse
I swear on my virginity; I already told her to come. Juliet! Foolish Child! Where are you?

(Enter Juliet.)

Juliet
What is it? Who calls me now?

Nurse
Your mother is asking for you.

Juliet
Yes, mother? What do you want?

Lady Capulet
Hold on. Nurse, can you give us some privacy. Wait, on second thought, stay. You know my daughter as well as me.

Nurse
I've know her since the hour she was born.

Lady Capulet
Then you know she is only thirteen.

Nurse
I would bet fourteen teeth, if I had that

Lady Capulet
Nurse, where's my daughter? call her forth to me.

Nurse
Now, by my maidenhea,--at twelve year old,-- I bade her come.--What, lamb! what ladybird!-- God forbid!--where's this girl?--what, Juliet!

[Enter Juliet.]

Juliet
How now, who calls?

Nurse
Your mother.

Juliet
Madam, I am here. What is your will?

Lady Capulet
This is the matter,--Nurse, give leave awhile, We must talk in secret: nurse, come back again; I have remember'd me, thou's hear our counsel. Thou knowest my daughter's of a pretty age.

Nurse
Faith, I can tell her age unto an hour.

Lady Capulet
She's not fourteen.

Nurse
I'll lay fourteen of my teeth,-- And yet, to

many, she is only thirteen. How long before August 1st?

Lady Capulet
Two weeks and a few days.

Nurse
She will be fourteen on August 1st. My daughter, Susan, God rest her soul, would be the same age. Susan was too good for me, so God called her home. So, Juliet will be fourteen on August 1st. She will be able to be married then. I remember the earthquake, only eleven years ago, when she was weaned. I will never forget it. I had just put something bitter-tasting on my breast while sitting under the dove-house wall, and she was struggling to nurse. The earth began to shake and we took off. She could already stand alone and run a little, for the day before she had fallen and bumped her head. My husband, God rest his soul, loved the child. He picked her up and said, "Did you fall on your face? You will fall in love when you are older, won't you?" I swear, she said, "Yes." Just like that, she stopped crying and said, "Yes." I'll never forget it.

my teen be it spoken, I have but four,--
She is not fourteen. How long is it now
To Lammas-tide?

Lady Capulet
A fortnight and odd days.

Nurse
Even or odd, of all days in the year, Come Lammas-eve at night shall she be fourteen. Susan and she,--God rest all Christian souls!-- Were of an age: well, Susan is with God; She was too good for me:--but, as I said, On Lammas-eve at night shall she be fourteen; That shall she, marry; I remember it well. 'Tis since the earthquake now eleven years; And she was wean'd,--I never shall forget it--, Of all the days of the year, upon that day: For I had then laid wormwood to my dug, Sitting in the sun under the dove-house wall; My lord and you were then at Mantua: Nay, I do bear a brain:--but, as I said, When it did taste the wormwood on the nipple Of my dug and felt it bitter, pretty fool, To see it tetchy, and fall out with the dug! Shake, quoth the dove-house: 'twas no need, I trow, To bid me trudge. And since that time it is eleven years; For then she could stand alone; nay, by the rood She could have run and waddled all about; For even the day before, she broke her brow: And then my husband,--God be with his soul! 'A was a merry man,--took up the child: 'Yea,' quoth he, 'dost thou fall upon thy face? Thou wilt fall backward when thou hast more wit; Wilt thou not, Jule?' and, by my holidame, The pretty wretch left crying, and said 'Ay:' To see now how a jest shall come about! I warrant, an I should live a thousand yeas, I never should forget it; 'Wilt thou not, Jule?' quoth he; And, pretty fool, it stinted, and

Lady Capulet
Okay, Nurse! Be quiet.

Nurse
Yes ma'am. But, I can't stop laughing, thinking about Juliet crying and then stopping and saying, "Yes," with a big goose egg on her head. It was a terrible bump and she cried, but my husband scooped her up and asked, "You will fall in love one day, won't you?" Juliet stopped crying and said, "Yes."

Juliet
It's your turn to be quiet now, Nurse.

Nurse
I have done my best by you. You were the prettiest baby I ever nursed. I just hope I live to see you married one day.

Lady Capulet
Marriage, that is what I wanted to talk to you about. How do you feel about marriage, Juliet?

Juliet
I haven't really given it much thought.

Nurse
Haven't thought of marriage? As your nurse, I think you aren't very smart to not think about it.

Lady Capulet
Well, think of marriage now. Many girls your age are already married and having

said 'Ay.'

Lady Capulet
Enough of this; I pray thee hold thy peace.

Nurse
Yes, madam;--yet I cannot choose but laugh, To think it should leave crying, and say 'Ay:' And yet, I warrant, it had upon its brow A bump as big as a young cockerel's stone; A parlous knock; and it cried bitterly. 'Yea,' quoth my husband, 'fall'st upon thy face? Thou wilt fall backward when thou com'st to age; Wilt thou not, Jule?' it stinted, and said 'Ay.'

Juliet
And stint thou too, I pray thee, nurse, say I.

Nurse
Peace, I have done. God mark thee to his grace! Thou wast the prettiest babe that e'er I nurs'd: An I might live to see thee married once, I have my wish.

Lady Capulet
Marry, that marry is the very theme I came to talk of.--Tell me, daughter Juliet, How stands your disposition to be married?

Juliet
It is an honour that I dream not of.

Nurse
An honour!--were not I thine only nurse, I would say thou hadst suck'd wisdom from thy teat.

Lady Capulet
Well, think of marriage now: younger than you, Here in Verona, ladies of

families. I was your mother at thirteen. But to get to the point, the valiant Paris seeks your hand in marriage.

Nurse
A man, Juliet, and what a man. He's a hunk!

Lady Capulet
He is handsome.

Nurse
He is a spiritual man, too.

Lady Capulet
So, what do you think? Do you think you could love him? He is coming to the party tonight. Take a look at him and consider if he would make a good husband. You two would make a beautiful couple, and you have nothing to lose.

Nurse
Nothing to lose and everything to gain. Like a baby!

Lady Capulet
Do you think you could love Paris?

Juliet

esteem, Are made already mothers: by my count I was your mother much upon these years That you are now a maid. Thus, then, in brief;-- The valiant Paris seeks you for his love.

Nurse
A man, young lady! lady, such a man As all the world--why he's a man of wax.

Lady Capulet
Verona's summer hath not such a flower.

Nurse
Nay, he's a flower, in faith, a very flower.

Lady Capulet
What say you? can you love the gentleman? This night you shall behold him at our feast; Read o'er the volume of young Paris' face, And find delight writ there with beauty's pen; Examine every married lineament, And see how one another lends content; And what obscur'd in this fair volume lies Find written in the margent of his eyes. This precious book of love, this unbound lover, To beautify him, only lacks a cover: The fish lives in the sea; and 'tis much pride For fair without the fair within to hide: That book in many's eyes doth share the glory, That in gold clasps locks in the golden story; So shall you share all that he doth possess, By having him, making yourself no less.

Nurse
No less! nay, bigger; women grow by men

Lady Capulet
Speak briefly, can you like of Paris' love?

Juliet

I'll take a look at him, but I cannot promise you I will fall in love.

(Enter a Servant.)

Servant
The guests have arrived and the food is being served. People are asking for Juliet and cursing the Nurse. It is a little chaotic, so I must ask you to come along.

Lady Capulet
I am coming. Juliet, the count is waiting.

Nurse
Go, Juliet. Seek a husband and find happiness.

(Exit all.)

I'll look to like, if looking liking move:
But no more deep will I endart mine eye
Than your consent gives strength to make it fly.

[Enter a Servant.]

Servant
Madam, the guests are come, supper served up, you called, my young lady asked for, the nurse cursed in the pantry, and everything in extremity. I must hence to wait; I beseech you, follow straight.

Lady Capulet
We follow thee. [Exit Servant.]-- Juliet, the county stays.

Nurse
Go, girl, seek happy nights to happy days.

[Exeunt.]

Scene IV: A street.

(Enter Romeo, Mercutio, Benvolio, with five or six Maskers, masked party-goers who dance, Torch-bearers, and others.)

Romeo What are we going to say, if asked why we're here? Or, are we just going to crash the party?	**Romeo** What, shall this speech be spoke for our excuse? Or shall we on without apology?
Benvolio No one explains their reasoning for going to a party anymore. It's not like we are going in dressed up as Cupid with a bow and arrow, or scaring ladies like a scarecrow. We are just going to go in there and dance. Let them take it as they wish, and then, we will be gone.	**Benvolio** The date is out of such prolixity: We'll have no Cupid hoodwink'd with a scarf, Bearing a Tartar's painted bow of lath, Scaring the ladies like a crow-keeper; Nor no without-book prologue, faintly spoke After the prompter, for our entrance: But, let them measure us by what they will, We'll measure them a measure, and be gone.
Romeo Give me a torch. I don't want any part of your dance. I am too sad, so I will carry the light.	**Romeo** Give me a torch,--I am not for this ambling; Being but heavy, I will bear the light.
Mercutio But, you must dance.	**Mercutio** Nay, gentle Romeo, we must have you dance.
Romeo No way! My sadness weighs me down too much to be light on my feet.	**Romeo** Not I, believe me: you have dancing shoes, With nimble soles; I have a soul of lead So stakes me to the ground I cannot move.
Mercutio Come on, Romeo, you are a lover. Like Cupid with his wings, soar above the ground.	**Mercutio** You are a lover; borrow Cupid's wings, And soar with them above a common bound.

Romeo

Cupid. He is the reason for my sadness. I am too sorrowful to fly. My sadness would make me sink to the ground.

Mercutio

Don't blame love for your depression, because love is a tender thing, light and wonderful.

Romeo

Love a tender thing, ha! Love is rude and boisterous, and pricks like a thorn.

Mercutio

Well, if love is rough with you, then you be rough with love. Use your prick and beat love back. Give me my mask. What do I care if someone sees me? (Puts on mask.) Let this mask transform my face.

Benvolio

Come on, let's go. As soon as we're in, start dancing.

Romeo

Give me the torch. You guys go ahead and I'll watch. I just am not up to dancing.

Mercutio

You are being a bore. Let us help you overcome the sadness that drowns you. Come on, we're wasting daylight.

Romeo

I am too sore enpierced with his shaft To soar with his light feathers; and so bound, I cannot bound a pitch above dull woe: Under love's heavy burden do I sink.

Mercutio

And, to sink in it, should you burden love; Too great oppression for a tender thing.

Romeo

Is love a tender thing? it is too rough, Too rude, too boisterous; and it pricks like thorn.

Mercutio

If love be rough with you, be rough with love; Prick love for pricking, and you beat love down.-- Give me a case to put my visage in: [Putting on a mask.] A visard for a visard! what care I What curious eye doth quote deformities? Here are the beetle-brows shall blush for me.

Benvolio

Come, knock and enter; and no sooner in But every man betake him to his legs.

Romeo

A torch for me: let wantons, light of heart, Tickle the senseless rushes with their heels; For I am proverb'd with a grandsire phrase,-- I'll be a candle-holder and look on,-- The game was ne'er so fair, and I am done.

Mercutio

Tut, dun's the mouse, the constable's own word: If thou art dun, we'll draw thee from the mire Of this--sir-reverence--love, wherein thou stick'st Up to the ears.-- Come, we burn daylight, ho.

Romeo
No we're not; it's night.

Mercutio
It's just a figure of speech. I mean we are wasting time and our torches. Use your brain and figure it out.

Romeo
Like how we are using our brains by going to this party, uninvited.

Mercutio
What do you mean?

Romeo
I had a dream last night.

Mercutio
So what? I dreamed last night, too.

Romeo
Well, what was yours?

Mercutio
I dreamed dreamers are often full of crap!

Romeo
Dreamers lie in bed and dream of truthful things.

Mercutio
Hmm…Was someone in the bed with you like the harlot, Mab? She is the fairies' midwife. She is no bigger than the alderman's ring. She has a little chariot drawn by atoms and lands on men's noses while they are asleep. The wagon wheel spokes are made of spider legs and the cover is grasshoppers' wings. The reigns are made of spider webs and the harnesses, moonbeams. Her driver is a small gnat, and her wagon an empty

Romeo
Nay, that's not so.

Mercutio
I mean, sir, in delay We waste our lights in vain, like lamps by day. Take our good meaning, for our judgment sits Five times in that ere once in our five wits.

Romeo
And we mean well, in going to this mask; But 'tis no wit to go.

Mercutio
Why, may one ask?

Romeo
I dreamt a dream to-night.

Mercutio
And so did I.

Romeo
Well, what was yours?

Mercutio
That dreamers often lie.

Romeo
In bed asleep, while they do dream things true.

Mercutio
O, then, I see Queen Mab hath been with you. She is the fairies' midwife; and she comes In shape no bigger than an agate-stone On the fore-finger of an alderman, Drawn with a team of little atomies Athwart men's noses as they lie asleep: Her waggon-spokes made of long spinners' legs; The cover, of the wings of grasshoppers; The traces, of the smallest spider's web; The collars, of the moonshine's watery beams; Her whip, of

hazelnut made by a squirrel or grub worm. She rides every night to lovers' beds and makes them dream of love. She makes young girls dream of curtsies, and lawyers money. Old ladies dream of kisses and priests dream of big tithes. She drives over the soldier's neck, and he dreams of murdering his enemies and the sound of drums going into battle, which scares him into waking. He says a prayer or two before going back to sleep. Mab is the one who plaits the horses' manes at night, and casts a spell of doom on anyone who untangles it. She is the one who gives good dreams to virgins, teaching them how to lay with a man…

cricket's bone; the lash, of film; Her waggoner, a small grey-coated gnat, Not half so big as a round little worm Prick'd from the lazy finger of a maid: Her chariot is an empty hazel-nut, Made by the joiner squirrel or old grub, Time out o' mind the fairies' coachmakers. And in this state she gallops night by night Through lovers' brains, and then they dream of love; O'er courtiers' knees, that dream on court'sies straight; O'er lawyers' fingers, who straight dream on fees; O'er ladies' lips, who straight on kisses dream,-- Which oft the angry Mab with blisters plagues, Because their breaths with sweetmeats tainted are: Sometime she gallops o'er a courtier's nose, And then dreams he of smelling out a suit; And sometime comes she with a tithe-pig's tail, Tickling a parson's nose as 'a lies asleep, Then dreams he of another benefice: Sometime she driveth o'er a soldier's neck, And then dreams he of cutting foreign throats, Of breaches, ambuscadoes, Spanish blades, Of healths five fathom deep; and then anon Drums in his ear, at which he starts and wakes; And, being thus frighted, swears a prayer or two, And sleeps again. This is that very Mab That plats the manes of horses in the night; And bakes the elf-locks in foul sluttish hairs, Which, once untangled, much misfortune bodes: This is the hag, when maids lie on their backs, That presses them, and learns them first to bear, Making them women of good carriage: This is she,--

Romeo
Enough, Mercutio. You are a babbling idiot.

Mercutio
Sure, I talk about dreams, which are a

Romeo
Peace, peace, Mercutio, peace, Thou talk'st of nothing.

Mercutio
True, I talk of dreams, Which are the

waste of time, the product of idle minds. They are meaningless and can no more predict the future than we can predict the wind.

Benvolio
You both are blowing wind and making us late.

Romeo
Going at all would be too early for me. I have a bad feeling about this. But, what do I care? Let's go gentleman.

Benvolio
Play the drum.

(Exit all.)

children of an idle brain, Begot of nothing but vain fantasy; Which is as thin of substance as the air, And more inconstant than the wind, who wooes Even now the frozen bosom of the north, And, being anger'd, puffs away from thence, Turning his face to the dew-dropping south.

Benvolio
This wind you talk of blows us from ourselves: Supper is done, and we shall come too late.

Romeo
I fear, too early: for my mind misgives Some consequence, yet hanging in the stars, Shall bitterly begin his fearful date With this night's revels; and expire the term Of a despised life, clos'd in my breast, By some vile forfeit of untimely death: But He that hath the steerage of my course Direct my sail!--On, lusty gentlemen!

Benvolio
Strike, drum.

[Exeunt.]

Scene V: A hall in the Capulet's house

(Musicians waiting. Enter Servants.)

First Servant Where's Potpan, that lazy rascal. He is shirking his duties again!	**1 Servant** Where's Potpan, that he helps not to take away? he shift a trencher! he scrape a trencher!
Second Servant It's a bad thing when the only one to do the cleaning is dirty.	**2 Servant** When good manners shall lie all in one or two men's hands, and they unwash'd too, 'tis a foul thing.
First Servant Take away the stools and put the plates away, good man. Also save me a piece of candy if you love me. Let the porter call in Susan Grindstone and Nell. Antony! And Potpan!	**1 Servant** Away with the join-stools, remove the court-cupboard, look to the plate:--good thou, save me a piece of marchpane; and as thou loves me, let the porter let in Susan Grindstone and Nell.-- Antony! and Potpan!
Second Servant Okay, I'm ready.	**2 Servant** Ay, boy, ready.
First Servant They are calling for you in the dancing hall.	**1 Servant** You are looked for and called for, asked for and sought for in the great chamber.
Second Servant How can I be in here and in there, too? Happy boys, the one who lives the longest can have it all.	**2 Servant** We cannot be here and there too.-- Cheerly, boys; be brisk awhile, and the longer liver take all.
(They retire behind.)	[They retire behind.]
(Enter Capulet with his cousin, guests, and dancers.)	[Enter Capulet, &c. with the Guests the Maskers.]
Capulet Welcome ladies and gentleman. Prepare	**Capulet** Welcome, gentlemen! ladies that have

to dance if you do not have corns on your feet. Which of you ladies will dance with me? Whoever denies me, I'll swear you have corns. Here I come. Welcome, gentleman. (To the dancers.) I remember the day when I wore a mask and whispered tales in the ladies' ears. But, that time is gone. Come, let us dance. Musicians play.

(Music plays and they dance.)

We need more light and remove the tables. Put the fire out, because it is too hot in here. Come cousin, let us sit. Our dancing days are behind us. How long has it been since we danced at a party like this?

Cousin
I swear it's been thirty years.

Capulet
It can't be that long ago. It was at the wedding of Lucentio. That has been twenty-five years ago.

Cousin
It's been longer than that. His son is at least thirty.

Capulet
No way; his son was a minor just two years ago.

Romeo
(To a servant.) Who is that lady with the knight?

their toes Unplagu'd with corns will have a bout with you.-- Ah ha, my mistresses! which of you all Will now deny to dance? she that makes dainty, she, I'll swear hath corns; am I come near you now? Welcome, gentlemen! I have seen the day That I have worn a visard; and could tell A whispering tale in a fair lady's ear, Such as would please;--'tis gone, 'tis gone, 'tis gone: You are welcome, gentlemen!-- Come, musicians, play. A hall--a hall! give room! and foot it, girls.-- [Music plays, and they dance.] More light, you knaves; and turn the tables up, And quench the fire, the room is grown too hot.-- Ah, sirrah, this unlook'd-for sport comes well. Nay, sit, nay, sit, good cousin Capulet; For you and I are past our dancing days; How long is't now since last yourself and I Were in a mask?

2 Capulet
By'r Lady, thirty years.

Capulet
What, man! 'tis not so much, 'tis not so much: 'Tis since the nuptial of Lucentio, Come Pentecost as quickly as it will, Some five-and-twenty years; and then we mask'd.

2 Capulet
'Tis more, 'tis more: his son is elder, sir; His son is thirty.

Capulet
Will you tell me that? His son was but a ward two years ago.

Romeo
What lady is that, which doth enrich the hand Of yonder knight?

Servant I don't know, sir.	**Servant** I know not, sir.
Romeo Like the light of the torch, she brings light to my eyes. She is as beautiful as a jewel in the ear of an Ethiopian. She stands out like a dove among crows. I will watch her and hope to touch her hand. Have I ever been in love before? My eyes have lied to me, because I have never seen anyone so beautiful.	**Romeo** O, she doth teach the torches to burn bright! It seems she hangs upon the cheek of night Like a rich jewel in an Ethiop's ear; Beauty too rich for use, for earth too dear! So shows a snowy dove trooping with crows As yonder lady o'er her fellows shows. The measure done, I'll watch her place of stand And, touching hers, make blessed my rude hand. Did my heart love till now? forswear it, sight! For I ne'er saw true beauty till this night.
Tybalt I know that voice. You are a Montague. (To a page.) Fetch me my sword. How dare he come to the house of Capulet? For that grievance, I will kill him.	**Tybalt** This, by his voice, should be a Montague.-- Fetch me my rapier, boy:--what, dares the slave Come hither, cover'd with an antic face, To fleer and scorn at our solemnity? Now, by the stock and honour of my kin, To strike him dead I hold it not a sin.
Capulet What's going on, Tybalt? Why are you so angry?	**Capulet** Why, how now, kinsman! wherefore storm you so?
Tybalt Uncle, a Montague, our enemy is here. He has crashed our party to destroy our fun.	**Tybalt** Uncle, this is a Montague, our foe; A villain, that is hither come in spite, To scorn at our solemnity this night.
Capulet Is it young Romeo?	**Capulet** Young Romeo, is it?
Tybalt It is, that little villain.	**Tybalt** 'Tis he, that villain, Romeo.
Capulet Calm down then. He is not bothering anyone. He is favored in the city of Verona. It would not look well if we	**Capulet** Content thee, gentle coz, let him alone, He bears him like a portly gentleman; And, to say truth, Verona brags of him To be a

insulted him. Be patient and leave him alone, if you have any respect for me. This is no way to behave at a party. Have a good time.

Tybalt
I am behaving exactly the way I should with a villain in my presence. I will not have him crashing our party.

Capulet
You will have it, if I say you will. Who is the master here, you? You'll not have it, and make a scene at my party among my guests. I don't think so, you trouble-maker.

Tybalt
Why? That is a shame!

Capulet
Get out of my face, you rude boy before your actions bring harm to you. How dare you contradict me? It is time for you to grow up. (To the guests) Having a good time? Wonderful. (To Tybalt) Be quiet or I'll make you shut up. (To the guests) Have a good time.

Tybalt
I will abide by my uncle this time, although my anger makes me tremble, but I will not forget what Romeo has done. What he thinks is a fun trick now, will not be so funny when I get through with him.

(Exit.)

virtuous and well-govern'd youth: I would not for the wealth of all the town Here in my house do him disparagement: Therefore be patient, take no note of him,-- It is my will; the which if thou respect, Show a fair presence and put off these frowns, An ill-beseeming semblance for a feast.

Tybalt
It fits, when such a villain is a guest: I'll not endure him.

Capulet
He shall be endur'd: What, goodman boy!--I say he shall;--go to; Am I the master here, or you? go to. You'll not endure him!--God shall mend my soul, You'll make a mutiny among my guests! You will set cock-a-hoop! you'll be the man!

Tybalt
Why, uncle, 'tis a shame.

Capulet
Go to, go to! You are a saucy boy. Is't so, indeed?-- This trick may chance to scathe you,--I know what: You must contrary me! marry, 'tis time.-- Well said, my hearts!--You are a princox; go: Be quiet, or--More light, more light!--For shame! I'll make you quiet. What!--cheerly, my hearts.

Tybalt
Patience perforce with wilful choler meeting Makes my flesh tremble in their different greeting. I will withdraw: but this intrusion shall, Now seeming sweet, convert to bitter gall.

[Exit.]

Romeo
(To Juliet.) If you find my rough hand offensive, let me offer you two smooth lips to kiss.

Juliet
Boy, I do not find your hand rough offensive. Doesn't everyone have hands? Holding hands is the nearest thing to kissing. Palm to palm, instead of lip to lip.

Romeo
Doesn't everyone have lips, too?

Juliet
Yes, but lips have many uses, like praying.

Romeo
Then, let lips do what hands do. I pray you grant me a kiss or I will lose my faith.

Juliet
That will not make you lose your faith.

Romeo
Then don't move. Stay still while I kiss you, and my sin will be purged.

(They kiss.)

Juliet
Am I a sinner now? Have you passed on your sin to me?

Romeo
Because you kissed me? Well, let me take my sin back.

Romeo
[To Juliet.] If I profane with my unworthiest hand This holy shrine, the gentle fine is this,-- My lips, two blushing pilgrims, ready stand To smooth that rough touch with a tender kiss.

Juliet
Good pilgrim, you do wrong your hand too much, Which mannerly devotion shows in this; For saints have hands that pilgrims' hands do touch, And palm to palm is holy palmers' kiss.

Romeo
Have not saints lips, and holy palmers too?

Juliet
Ay, pilgrim, lips that they must use in prayer.

Romeo
O, then, dear saint, let lips do what hands do; They pray, grant thou, lest faith turn to despair.

Juliet
Saints do not move, though grant for prayers' sake.

Romeo
Then move not while my prayer's effect I take. Thus from my lips, by thine my sin is purg'd. [Kissing her.]

Juliet
Then have my lips the sin that they have took.

Romeo
Sin from my lips? O trespass sweetly urg'd! Give me my sin again.

(They kiss again.)

Juliet
You kiss perfectly!

Nurse
Madam, your mother wants to talk with you.

Romeo
(To Nurse.) Who is her mother?

Nurse
Young man, her mother is the lady who lives in this house. She is a good lady, wise and virtuous. I am her daughter's nurse, the girl you were talking to. He, who wins her heart, will have it made.

Romeo
Is she a Capulet? Oh my God! I have just fallen for the daughter of my enemy.

Benvolio
Come on; let's go before it is too late.

Romeo
I'm afraid it is already too late.

Capulet
Don't go yet, gentlemen. We still have more food coming. Is that so? Well, thank you all. Thank you for coming. We need more light over here. Let's go to bed. (To Cousin.) I did not know it was so late. I'm going to bed.

(Exit all but Juliet and Nurse.)

Juliet
Come here, Nurse. Who was that young

Juliet
You kiss by the book.

Nurse
Madam, your mother craves a word with you.

Romeo
What is her mother?

Nurse
Marry, bachelor, Her mother is the lady of the house. And a good lady, and a wise and virtuous: I nurs'd her daughter that you talk'd withal; I tell you, he that can lay hold of her Shall have the chinks.

Romeo
Is she a Capulet? O dear account! my life is my foe's debt.

Benvolio
Away, be gone; the sport is at the best.

Romeo
Ay, so I fear; the more is my unrest.

Capulet
Nay, gentlemen, prepare not to be gone;
We have a trifling foolish banquet towards.-- Is it e'en so? why then, I thank you all; I thank you, honest gentlemen; good-night.-- More torches here!--Come on then, let's to bed. Ah, sirrah [to 2 Capulet], by my fay, it waxes late; I'll to my rest.

[Exeunt all but Juliet and Nurse.]

Juliet
Come hither, nurse. What is yond

gentleman?

Nurse
He is the son and heir of old Tiberio.

Juliet
Not him; the one who is going out the door.

Nurse
I think his name is Petruchio.

Juliet
No, not him either. Who was the one that would not dance?

Nurse
I don't know his name.

Juliet
Well go find out, and ask if he is married. I'm likely to die if I don't marry him.

Nurse
His name is Romeo, and he is a Montague. He is the only son of your worst enemy.

Juliet
Oh no! The only man I love is the son of the only man I hate. Why couldn't I have known this before? Unfair love, why must I love someone I hate?

Nurse
What are you talking about?

Juliet
Oh nothing.

(Someone calls for Juliet.)

Nurse

gentleman?

Nurse
The son and heir of old Tiberio.

Juliet
What's he that now is going out of door?

Nurse
Marry, that, I think, be young Petruchio.

Juliet
What's he that follows there, that would not dance?

Nurse
I know not.

Juliet
Go ask his name: if he be married, My grave is like to be my wedding-bed.

Nurse
His name is Romeo, and a Montague; The only son of your great enemy.

Juliet
My only love sprung from my only hate! Too early seen unknown, and known too late! Prodigious birth of love it is to me, That I must love a loathed enemy.

Nurse
What's this? What's this?

Juliet
A rhyme I learn'd even now Of one I danc'd withal.

[One calls within, 'Juliet.']

Nurse

Here we are. Come on let's go. The guests are all gone.

(Exit all.)

(Enter Chorus.)

Chorus
Old desire dies,
And young affection takes its place;
Rosaline, whom Romeo groaned for,
Has been replaced by Juliet.
Now Romeo's love is returned;
Both falling for looks alone.
But he loves the enemy;
And she has fallen for her foe.
Thus, he is forbidden to pursue her;
And she cannot sneak away to meet him.
But passion makes them powerful;
And chance favors them to meet.
They test extreme danger,
For extreme pleasure.

Anon, anon! Come, let's away; the strangers all are gone.

[Exeunt.]

[Enter Chorus.]

Chorus
Now old desire doth in his deathbed lie,
And young affection gapes to be his heir;
That fair for which love groan'd for, and would die, With tender Juliet match'd, is now not fair. Now Romeo is belov'd, and loves again, Alike bewitched by the charm of looks; But to his foe suppos'd he must complain, And she steal love's sweet bait from fearful hooks: Being held a foe, he may not have access To breathe such vows as lovers us'd to swear; And she as much in love, her means much less To meet her new beloved anywhere: But passion lends them power, time means, to meet, Tempering extremities with extreme sweet.

[Exit.]

Act II

Scene I: An open place adjoining Capulet's garden.

Romeo
My heart is here. Where else can I be?

(He climbs the wall and leaps down within it.)

(Enter Benvolio and Mercutio.)

Benvolio
Romeo! Where are you?

Mercutio
He is too smart to be here. He must have gone home and is in bed by now.

Benvolio
I saw him run this way and leap over this orchard wall. Call him, Mercutio.

Mercutio
I will conjure him up with my magic powers. Romeo! Oh, Passionate Lover! If you are there let us hear a sigh or some rhyme and I will be satisfied. If you are in a compromising situation, just cry out, "Ah me! Or, say love and dove. Cry out to Venus, the goddess of love or to her red-headed son, Cupid, who shoots so well. Romeo does not hear me. He does not move. He must be dead, and I must bring him magically forth. I call you by the name of the bright-eyed Rosaline with the high forehead and red lips, the fine foot, straight leg, and quivering thigh, and the area between those thighs. Appear before us now!

Romeo
Can I go forward when my heart is here? Turn back, dull earth, and find thy centre out.

[He climbs the wall and leaps down within it.]

[Enter Benvolio and Mercutio.]

Benvolio
Romeo! my cousin Romeo!

Mercutio
He is wise; And, on my life, hath stol'n him home to bed.

Benvolio
He ran this way, and leap'd this orchard wall: Call, good Mercutio.

Mercutio
Nay, I'll conjure too.-- Romeo! humours! madman! passion! lover! Appear thou in the likeness of a sigh: Speak but one rhyme, and I am satisfied; Cry but 'Ah me!' pronounce but Love and dove; Speak to my gossip Venus one fair word, One nickname for her purblind son and heir, Young auburn Cupid, he that shot so trim When King Cophetua lov'd the beggar-maid!-- He heareth not, he stirreth not, he moveth not; The ape is dead, and I must conjure him.-- I conjure thee by Rosaline's bright eyes, By her high forehead and her scarlet lip, By her fine foot, straight leg, and quivering thigh, And the demesnes that there adjacent lie, That in thy likeness thou appear to us!

Benvolio

If he hears you, he will be mad.

Mercutio

He shouldn't be. I am speaking truthfully when I conjure him in the name of his beloved. Now, if I were conjuring a man for her, then he should be angry.

Benvolio

Come on. He has hidden himself among these trees. He is blinded by love so he longs for the dark.

Mercutio

If love were blind, it would never find someone. He sits under a tree and wishes his love were its fruit that looks like a woman's private parts. Good night, Romeo. I'm going to my house, to my bed. This field is too cold for me to sleep upon. Come on. Are you ready to go?

Benvolio

I'm ready. It's pointless to try and find him, if he does not want to be found.

(Exit all.)

Benvolio

An if he hear thee, thou wilt anger him.

Mercutio

This cannot anger him: 'twould anger him To raise a spirit in his mistress' circle, Of some strange nature, letting it there stand Till she had laid it, and conjur'd it down; That were some spite: my invocation Is fair and honest, and, in his mistress' name, I conjure only but to raise up him.

Benvolio

Come, he hath hid himself among these trees, To be consorted with the humorous night: Blind is his love, and best befits the dark.

Mercutio

If love be blind, love cannot hit the mark. Now will he sit under a medlar tree, And wish his mistress were that kind of fruit As maids call medlars when they laugh alone.-- Romeo, good night.--I'll to my truckle-bed; This field-bed is too cold for me to sleep: Come, shall we go?

Benvolio

Go then; for 'tis in vain To seek him here that means not to be found.

[Exeunt.]

Scene II: Capulet's garden.

(Enter Romeo)

Romeo
He laughs at me, but he has never been scarred by love.

(Juliet appears above at a window.)

Whose soft light in the window do I see? Is it the rising sun of the east or my Juliet? Arise fair sun, and kill the jealous moon. The moon is jealous of your beauty, so do not be a maid of the moon. Her virginity is intact and this makes her green with envy. So do not be a fool, cast off your love—It is my lady; Oh, my love! I wish she knew how I love her! She is talking, but I can't hear her words. Her eyes are weary, so I will comfort her. But, maybe she would be offended if I try. Her eyes twinkle like two of the fairest stars in all the heavens. How I long to be reflected in those spheres. It appears the stars have traded places with her eyes, but the brightness of her cheek would outshine the stars. Like daylight, brighter than a lamp, she brightens the night so that the birds think it is day. Now, she leans her cheek upon her hand, and I wish I were a glove upon that hand, touching her cheek.

Juliet
Ah me!

Romeo
She speaks: Please speak again, bright angel? You are as glorious as an angel, flying through the air, upon which mortal

Romeo
He jests at scars that never felt a wound.-- [Juliet appears above at a window.] But soft! what light through yonder window breaks? It is the east, and Juliet is the sun!-- Arise, fair sun, and kill the envious moon, Who is already sick and pale with grief, That thou her maid art far more fair than she: Be not her maid, since she is envious; Her vestal livery is but sick and green, And none but fools do wear it; cast it off.-- It is my lady; O, it is my love! O, that she knew she were!-- She speaks, yet she says nothing: what of that? Her eye discourses, I will answer it.-- I am too bold, 'tis not to me she speaks: Two of the fairest stars in all the heaven, Having some business, do entreat her eyes To twinkle in their spheres till they return. What if her eyes were there, they in her head? The brightness of her cheek would shame those stars, As daylight doth a lamp; her eyes in heaven Would through the airy region stream so bright That birds would sing and think it were not night.-- See how she leans her cheek upon her hand! O that I were a glove upon that hand, That I might touch that cheek!

Juliet
Ah me!

Romeo
She speaks:-- O, speak again, bright angel! for thou art As glorious to this night, being o'er my head, As is a winged

eyes gaze.

Juliet
Oh Romeo, Romeo! Where are you Romeo? Do not take the name of your father. Better yet, I will change my name, if you only swear your love to me.

Romeo
Do I dare speak or should I listen longer?

Juliet
It is only your name that is my enemy. Not you. What is a Montague? It is not a hand or foot, arm or face, or any other part of a man. Why couldn't you be someone besides a Montague! What is a name anyway? Wouldn't a rose smell just as sweet, if we called it something else? Wouldn't you be just as perfect, if your name was different? Exchange your name, Romeo, and I will give myself to you.

Romeo
I hope what you say is true. If you call me your lover, then I will change my name like I have been re-baptized.

Juliet
Who's out there? Who is listening to my private thoughts?

Romeo
I do not know what to call myself, since I hate my name, because it is offensive to you. If I saw it written on a piece of paper, I would tear it up.

messenger of heaven Unto the white-upturned wondering eyes Of mortals that fall back to gaze on him When he bestrides the lazy-pacing clouds And sails upon the bosom of the air.

Juliet
O Romeo, Romeo! wherefore art thou Romeo? Deny thy father and refuse thy name; Or, if thou wilt not, be but sworn my love, And I'll no longer be a Capulet.

Romeo
[Aside.] Shall I hear more, or shall I speak at this?

Juliet
'Tis but thy name that is my enemy;-- Thou art thyself, though not a Montague. What's Montague? It is nor hand, nor foot, Nor arm, nor face, nor any other part Belonging to a man. O, be some other name! What's in a name? that which we call a rose By any other name would smell as sweet; So Romeo would, were he not Romeo call'd, Retain that dear perfection which he owes Without that title:--Romeo, doff thy name; And for that name, which is no part of thee, Take all myself.

Romeo
I take thee at thy word: Call me but love, and I'll be new baptiz'd; Henceforth I never will be Romeo.

Juliet
What man art thou that, thus bescreen'd in night, So stumblest on my counsel?

Romeo
By a name I know not how to tell thee who I am: My name, dear saint, is hateful to myself, Because it is an enemy to thee. Had I it written, I would tear the word.

Juliet

Even though we have only just met, I know that voice. Aren't you Romeo, a Montague?

Romeo

Not any longer, if you don't want me to be.

Juliet

Why are you here? How did you get here? The orchard walls are high and hard to climb, and you will be killed, if you are discovered.

Romeo

On the wings of Cupid, I flew over those walls. Nothing could keep my love from you, because it gives me strength to do the unthinkable and courage to face your kinsmen.

Juliet

If they see you, they will kill you.

Romeo

A harsh look from you would kill me, but twenty of their swords cannot touch me.

Juliet

I would not have them find you for anything.

Romeo

The night hides me from their sight, but if you love me, who cares if they find me? I would rather die knowing you loved me than live without you.

Juliet

My ears have yet not drunk a hundred words Of that tongue's utterance, yet I know the sound; Art thou not Romeo, and a Montague?

Romeo

Neither, fair saint, if either thee dislike.

Juliet

How cam'st thou hither, tell me, and wherefore? The orchard walls are high and hard to climb; And the place death, considering who thou art, If any of my kinsmen find thee here.

Romeo

With love's light wings did I o'erperch these walls; For stony limits cannot hold love out: And what love can do, that dares love attempt; Therefore thy kinsmen are no let to me.

Juliet

If they do see thee, they will murder thee.

Romeo

Alack, there lies more peril in thine eye Than twenty of their swords: look thou but sweet, And I am proof against their enmity.

Juliet

I would not for the world they saw thee here.

Romeo

I have night's cloak to hide me from their sight; And, but thou love me, let them find me here. My life were better ended by their hate Than death prorogued, wanting of thy love.

Juliet
How did you find me?

Romeo
My love guided me here. Even though I am not a sailor, I would travel the furthest and most dangerous sea to find you.

Juliet
If the night did not hide my face, you would see me blush. I did not intend for you to hear my words. I could deny what I have said, but I can't. Do you love me? I know you will say "yes," and I will believe you. You might swear it, and turn out to be a liar. You know, they say the king of the gods, Jove, laughs when lovers lie to each other. So don't lie to me. If you love me, tell me, but don't think that I am easy. Perhaps, I should play hard-to-get, so you have to prove you love me. However, I'm not that kind of girl. I am truer than the one who acts evasive. I probably should have acted that way, but what I have said here tonight is genuine.

Romeo
Juliet, I swear by the moon that shines upon these fruit trees…

Juliet
By whose direction found'st thou out this place?

Romeo
By love, that first did prompt me to enquire; He lent me counsel, and I lent him eyes. I am no pilot; yet, wert thou as far As that vast shore wash'd with the furthest sea, I would adventure for such merchandise.

Juliet
Thou knowest the mask of night is on my face; Else would a maiden blush bepaint my cheek For that which thou hast heard me speak to-night. Fain would I dwell on form,fain, fain deny What I have spoke; but farewell compliment! Dost thou love me, I know thou wilt say Ay; And I will take thy word: yet, if thou swear'st, Thou mayst prove false; at lovers' perjuries, They say Jove laughs. O gentle Romeo, If thou dost love, pronounce it faithfully: Or if thou thinkest I am too quickly won, I'll frown, and be perverse, and say thee nay, So thou wilt woo: but else, not for the world. In truth, fair Montague, I am too fond; And therefore thou mayst think my 'haviour light: But trust me, gentleman, I'll prove more true Than those that have more cunning to be strange. I should have been more strange, I must confess, But that thou overheard'st, ere I was 'ware, My true-love passion: therefore pardon me; And not impute this yielding to light love, Which the dark night hath so discovered.

Romeo
Lady, by yonder blessed moon I swear, That tips with silver all these fruit-tree tops,--

Juliet
No, do not swear by the moon, because it is constantly changing. I don't want your love to be like the moon.

Romeo
What do you want me to swear by?

Juliet
You don't have to swear at all. Your word is good enough.

Romeo
Then I will swear by my heart…

Juliet
Do not swear at all. I can't take all of this tonight. It is too soon, too dangerous, too hurried. I do not want our love to be like lightning, quickly here and quickly gone. I want our love to be like the budding of a beautiful flower. So, good night. Good night and rest peacefully. I know I will.

Romeo
You can't leave me like this, so unsatisfied.

Juliet
How can I satisfy you tonight?

Romeo
Let's exchange lover's vows.

Juliet
I already vowed my love to you, but I would do it again, if I had to.

Juliet. O, swear not by the moon, the inconstant moon, That monthly changes in her circled orb, Lest that thy love prove likewise variable.

Romeo
What shall I swear by?

Juliet
Do not swear at all; Or if thou wilt, swear by thy gracious self, Which is the god of my idolatry, And I'll believe thee.

Romeo
If my heart's dear love,--

Juliet
Well, do not swear: although I joy in thee, I have no joy of this contract to-night; It is too rash, too unadvis'd, too sudden; Too like the lightning, which doth cease to be Ere one can say It lightens. Sweet, good night! This bud of love, by summer's ripening breath, May prove a beauteous flower when next we meet. Good night, good night! as sweet repose and rest Come to thy heart as that within my breast!

Romeo
O, wilt thou leave me so unsatisfied?

Juliet
What satisfaction canst thou have to-night?

Romeo
The exchange of thy love's faithful vow for mine.

Juliet
I gave thee mine before thou didst request it; And yet I would it were to give again.

Romeo
You would take back what you said?
Why?

Juliet
Only to give it to you again. My only
wish is for your love, which you have
given me. The more you love me, the
more love I have to give to you. Our love
is infinite. I hear someone inside, dear
love. Farewell! (Nurse calls from
inside.) Here I am, Nurse! (To Romeo.)
Sweet Montague, be true. Stay for a little
while. I will be right back.

(Exit.)

Romeo
What a great night! I am afraid that I am
dreaming, because this is too good to be
true.

(Enter Juliet above.)

Juliet
Listen, I only have a few minutes; then
you must leave. If you honestly love me
and want to marry me, send me word
tomorrow. I will send someone to bring
me the message. I will meet you
wherever and whenever you choose to
become your wife. Then, I will put my
future in your hands and follow you all
the days of my life.

Nurse
(From inside.) Madam!

Juliet
(To Nurse.) I am coming! (To Romeo.)
But if you do not mean what you say, I
beg you…

Romeo
Would'st thou withdraw it? for what
purpose, love?

Juliet
But to be frank and give it thee again. And
yet I wish but for the thing I have; My
bounty is as boundless as the sea, My love
as deep; the more I give to thee, The more
I have, for both are infinite. I hear some
noise within: dear love, adieu!-- [Nurse
calls within.] Anon, good nurse!--Sweet
Montague, be true. Stay but a little, I will
come again.

[Exit.]

Romeo
O blessed, blessed night! I am afeard,
Being in night, all this is but a dream, Too
flattering-sweet to be substantial.

[Enter Juliet above.]

Juliet
Three words, dear Romeo, and good night
indeed. If that thy bent of love be
honourable, Thy purpose marriage, send
me word to-morrow, By one that I'll
procure to come to thee, Where and what
time thou wilt perform the rite; And all
my fortunes at thy foot I'll lay And follow
thee, my lord, throughout the world.

Nurse
[Within.] Madam!

Juliet
I come anon.-- But if thou meanest not
well, I do beseech thee,--

Nurse (From inside.) Madam!	**Nurse** [Within.] Madam!
Juliet (To Nurse.) Okay, already. I'm coming! (To Romeo.) I beg you to leave. I will send someone tomorrow.	**Juliet** By-and-by I come:-- To cease thy suit and leave me to my grief: To-morrow will I send.
Romeo I will think of nothing else!	Romeo. So thrive my soul,--
Juliet Okay. Go. A thousand times goodnight!	**Juliet** A thousand times good night!
(Exit.)	[Exit.]
Romeo I do not want to leave you. It is a thousand times worse when you are not near. Lovers aren't meant to be separated like a schoolboy from his books. And, when they are, it is as terrible as having to go to school.	**Romeo** A thousand times the worse, to want thy light!-- Love goes toward love as schoolboys from their books; But love from love, towards school with heavy looks.
(Retiring slowly.) (Re-enter Juliet, above.)	[Retirong slowly.] [Re-enter Juliet, above.]
Juliet Psst, Romeo! Psst! Oh, I wish I could make a bird call to bring him back again. I am suffocating in this house. I wish I could find the place where Echo lives and make her repeat my Romeo's name.	**Juliet** Hist! Romeo, hist!--O for a falconer's voice To lure this tassel-gentle back again! Bondage is hoarse and may not speak aloud; Else would I tear the cave where Echo lies, And make her airy tongue more hoarse than mine With repetition of my Romeo's name.
Romeo My love, my soul is calling my name. Her voice is like music to my ears.	**Romeo** It is my soul that calls upon my name: How silver-sweet sound lovers' tongues by night, Like softest music to attending ears!
Juliet	**Juliet**

Romeo!

Romeo
My dear?

Juliet
What time do you want me to send my messenger?

Romeo
At nine o'clock.

Juliet
I will not fail. It feels like tomorrow is twenty years from now. I have forgotten why I called you back.

Romeo
Let me wait here till you remember.

Juliet
I will never remember with you standing there. All I can think about is how much I love you being here.

Romeo
Then, I will never leave. I will forget any other place but this.

Juliet
It is almost morning. You must go. I don't want you to, but you must. I don't want to be like the owner of a little pet bird that lets it freely hop around only to be pulled back in by a string.

Romeo
I wish I were your pet.

Juliet
Sweetie, so do I. However, I would probably smother you with my love. Good night, good night! Separating is so

Romeo!

Romeo
My dear?

Juliet
At what o'clock to-morrow Shall I send to thee?

Romeo
At the hour of nine.

Juliet
I will not fail: 'tis twenty years till then. I have forgot why I did call thee back.

Romeo
Let me stand here till thou remember it.

Juliet
I shall forget, to have thee still stand there, Remembering how I love thy company.

Romeo
And I'll still stay, to have thee still forget, Forgetting any other home but this.

Juliet
'Tis almost morning; I would have thee gone: And yet no farther than a wanton's bird; That lets it hop a little from her hand, Like a poor prisoner in his twisted gyves, And with a silk thread plucks it back again, So loving-jealous of his liberty.

Romeo
I would I were thy bird.

Juliet
Sweet, so would I: Yet I should kill thee with much cherishing. Good night, good night! parting is such sweet sorrow That I

hard, and it fills me with sorrow, but we must say good night until tomorrow.

(Exit.)

Romeo
Sleep peacefully tonight. I wish I could stay with you. I will go to my priest, tell him my story, and ask for his help.

(Exit all.)

shall say good night till it be morrow.

[Exit.]

Romeo
Sleep dwell upon thine eyes, peace in thy breast!-- Would I were sleep and peace, so sweet to rest! Hence will I to my ghostly father's cell, His help to crave and my dear hap to tell.

[Exit.]

Scene III: Friar Lawrence's cell

(Enter Friar Lawrence with a basket.)

Friar Lawrence	Friar
The dawn of morning smiles upon the frowns of night, streaking the eastern sky with light. Like a drunk, the darkness stumbles away. Now, before the sun comes up, heating up the earth, drying the dew, I must fill this basket with poisonous weeds and precious flowers. The earth is nature's mother and her tomb. From her womb, I will collect many different types of natural items that have medicinal qualities so helpful to her children. But, even good things can come to no good, if they are abused. This small flower smells so sweet, but if one were to eat it, their heart would cease to beat. Men, like this flower, possess both natures; good and evil. <div align="center">(Enter Romeo.)</div>	The grey-ey'd morn smiles on the frowning night, Chequering the eastern clouds with streaks of light; And flecked darkness like a drunkard reels From forth day's path and Titan's fiery wheels: Non, ere the sun advance his burning eye, The day to cheer and night's dank dew to dry, I must up-fill this osier cage of ours With baleful weeds and precious-juiced flowers. The earth, that's nature's mother, is her tomb; What is her burying gave, that is her womb: And from her womb children of divers kind We sucking on her natural bosom find; Many for many virtues excellent, None but for some, and yet all different. O, mickle is the powerful grace that lies In plants, herbs, stones, and their true qualities: For naught so vile that on the earth doth live But to the earth some special good doth give; Nor aught so good but, strain'd from that fair use, Revolts from true birth, stumbling on abuse: Virtue itself turns vice, being misapplied; And vice sometimes by action dignified. Within the infant rind of this small flower Poison hath residence, and medicine power: For this, being smelt, with that part cheers each part; Being tasted, slays all senses with the heart. Two such opposed kings encamp them still In man as well as herbs,--grace and rude will; And where the worser is predominant, Full soon the canker death eats up that plant. [Enter Romeo.]

Romeo Good morning, father!	**Romeo** Good morrow, father!
Friar Laurence May God bless you! What causes you to be in such a good mood? Why are you up so early? This hour is for old men who worry, not young men who should be living the care-free life. Are you unwell or have you not been to bed at all?	**Friar** Benedicite! What early tongue so sweet saluteth me?-- Young son, it argues a distemper'd head So soon to bid good morrow to thy bed: Care keeps his watch in every old man's eye, And where care lodges sleep will never lie; But where unbruised youth with unstuff'd brain Doth couch his limbs, there golden sleep doth reign: Therefore thy earliness doth me assure Thou art uprous'd with some distemperature; Or if not so, then here I hit it right,-- Our Romeo hath not been in bed to-night.
Romeo It is true. I haven't been to bed.	**Romeo** That last is true; the sweeter rest was mine.
Friar Laurence I pray you have not been with Rosaline.	**Friar** God pardon sin! wast thou with Rosaline?
Romeo No, I have not been with Rosaline. I am over her!	**Romeo** With Rosaline, my ghostly father? no; I have forgot that name, and that name's woe.
Friar Laurence That's good, my son, but where were you then?	**Friar** That's my good son: but where hast thou been then?
Romeo I'll tell you. I have been at the Capulet party. I have fallen in love and someone has fallen in love with me. And, you are just the person to help us out. I no longer carry any hatred, father, for the love of my life was once my enemy.	**Romeo** I'll tell thee ere thou ask it me again. I have been feasting with mine enemy; Where, on a sudden, one hath wounded me That's by me wounded. Both our remedies Within thy help and holy physic lies; I bear no hatred, blessed man; for, lo, My intercession likewise steads my foe.
Friar Laurence	**Friar**

I don't understand. Who are you talking about?

Romeo
I am talking about the fair daughter of rich Capulet. We are in love and want to get married. That is how you can help us. Perform the ceremony.

Friar Laurence
Holy Saint Francis! What a turnaround. Have you forgotten how much in love you were with Rosaline, and how you cried when she didn't return your feelings? I certainly have not. I'm afraid you are not being rational in saying you have changed. How can you expect a woman to fall in love with you when you are so wishy-washy?

Romeo
You have often rebuked me for loving Rosaline.

Friar Laurence
Not for loving her, my student, but being crazy about her.

Romeo

Be plain, good son, and homely in thy drift; Riddling confession finds but riddling shrift.

Romeo
Then plainly know my heart's dear love is set On the fair daughter of rich Capulet: As mine on hers, so hers is set on mine; And all combin'd, save what thou must combine By holy marriage: when, and where, and how We met, we woo'd, and made exchange of vow, I'll tell thee as we pass; but this I pray, That thou consent to marry us to-day.

Friar
Holy Saint Francis! what a change is here! Is Rosaline, that thou didst love so dear, So soon forsaken? young men's love, then, lies Not truly in their hearts, but in their eyes. Jesu Maria, what a deal of brine Hath wash'd thy sallow cheeks for Rosaline! How much salt water thrown away in waste, To season love, that of it doth not taste! The sun not yet thy sighs from heaven clears, Thy old groans ring yet in mine ancient ears; Lo, here upon thy cheek the stain doth sit Of an old tear that is not wash'd off yet: If e'er thou wast thyself, and these woes thine, Thou and these woes were all for Rosaline; And art thou chang'd? Pronounce this sentence then,-- Women may fall, when there's no strength in men.

Romeo
Thou chidd'st me oft for loving Rosaline.

Friar
For doting, not for loving, pupil mine.

Romeo

You told me to bury my love for her.

Friar Laurence
I did not mean for you to bury your love for her and replace it with another.

Romeo
Don't start scolding me for who I love now. This girl feels the same for me as I do for her. Rosaline didn't.

Friar Laurence
Oh, Rosaline knew how you felt about her, and she knew you didn't know anything about love. However, I think I can be of assistance. Come with me. Perhaps, this marriage will bring an end to the feuds held by your families.

Romeo
Good, let's go. I am in a hurry.

Friar Laurence
But, let's go slowly and wisely, for those who rush into such ceremonies stumble and fall.

(They exit.)

And bad'st me bury love.

Friar
Not in a grave To lay one in, another out to have.

Romeo
I pray thee chide not: she whom I love now Doth grace for grace and love for love allow; The other did not so.

Friar
O, she knew well Thy love did read by rote, that could not spell. But come, young waverer, come go with me, In one respect I'll thy assistant be; For this alliance may so happy prove, To turn your households' rancour to pure love.

Romeo
O, let us hence; I stand on sudden haste.

Friar
Wisely, and slow; they stumble that run fast.

[Exeunt.]

Scene IV: A street.

(Enter Benvolio and Mercutio.)

Mercutio Where in the devil is Romeo? Did he not come home last night?	**Mercutio** Where the devil should this Romeo be?-- Came he not home to-night?
Benvolio I spoke with his servant this morning, and he did not go to his father's house.	**Benvolio** Not to his father's; I spoke with his man.
Mercutio Rosaline is a hard-hearted wench. I'm afraid she is going to drive him mad.	**Mercutio** Ah, that same pale hard-hearted wench, that Rosaline, Torments him so that he will sure run mad.
Benvolio Tybalt, old Capulet's nephew, sent a letter to Romeo's father's house.	**Benvolio** Tybalt, the kinsman to old Capulet, Hath sent a letter to his father's house.
Mercutio A challenge for his life, I suppose.	**Mercutio** A challenge, on my life.
Benvolio Yes, and Romeo will accept the challenge.	**Benvolio** Romeo will answer it.
Mercutio Anyone who can write may answer a letter.	**Mercutio** Any man that can write may answer a letter.
Benvolio Romeo won't shy away from Tybalt. He will be enraged at being dared.	**Benvolio** Nay, he will answer the letter's master, how he dares, being dared.
Mercutio Oh well. Poor Romeo is as good as dead, stabbed by the white wench's black eye, shot through the ear with a love song, and pierced through the heart by Cupid's bow.	**Mercutio** Alas, poor Romeo, he is already dead! stabbed with a white wench's black eye; shot through the ear with a love song; the very pin of his heart cleft with the blind

He is no match for Tybalt.

Benvolio
Why not? What's so great about Tybalt?

Mercutio
He is certainly charming, but he is also brutal. In three strikes, his opponents are dead. He is a well-studied fencist. He knows passado, the forward thrust, punto reverso, the backhand thrust, and hay, the thrust to the heart.

Benvolio
He knows what?

Mercutio
I hate people like Tybalt with their fancy way of talking, "What a good sword, what a very tall man, what a good whore!" Why should we have to put up with men like him who dress in high fashion and say, "Pardon me?" They cannot even sit down without groaning about an ache in their bones.

Benvolio
Here comes Romeo! Here comes Romeo!

Mercutio
He looks dried up like a fish. He looks ready to drop! Oh, what women can do to men. Like Laura, the kitchen slave, the shabbily-dressed Dido, Cleopatra, the gypsy, the sluts, Helen and Hero, or

---

bow-boy's butt-shaft: and is he a man to encounter Tybalt?

Benvolio
Why, what is Tybalt?

Mercutio
More than prince of cats, I can tell you. O, he's the courageous captain of compliments. He fights as you sing prick-song--keeps time, distance, and proportion; rests me his minim rest, one, two, and the third in your bosom: the very butcher of a silk button, a duellist, a duellist; a gentleman of the very first house,--of the first and second cause: ah, the immortal passado! the punto reverso! the hay.--

Benvolio
The what?

Mercutio
The pox of such antic, lisping, affecting fantasticoes; these new tuners of accents!--'By Jesu, a very good blade!--a very tall man!--a very good whore!'--Why, is not this a lamentable thing, grandsire, that we should be thus afflicted with these strange flies, these fashion-mongers, these pardonnez-moi's, who stand so much on the new form that they cannot sit at ease on the old bench? O, their bons, their bons!

Benvolio
Here comes Romeo, here comes Romeo!

Mercutio
Without his roe, like a dried herring.--O flesh, flesh, how art thou fishified!--Now is he for the numbers that Petrarch flowed in: Laura, to his lady, was but a kitchen wench,--marry, she had a better love to

Thisbe with her gray eyes.

(Enter Romeo.)

Bon jour, Signor Romeo. There is a French salutation to match your sloppy French look. You certainly gave us the slip last night.

Romeo
Good morning to both of you. How did I give you the slip?

Mercutio
The slip, sir. You don't understand the meaning of the word?

Romeo
I beg your pardon, Mercutio. I had important business to take care of so please forgive my bad manners.

Mercutio
(Referring to sex.) Was it so important that you had to "stretch your legs?"

Romeo
You mean did I have to "curtsy?"

Mercutio
Exactly.

Romeo
Well, that's one way to say it politely.

Mercutio
I am nothing but polite, fresh like a virgin's untouched body.

Romeo

be-rhyme her; Dido, a dowdy; Cleopatra, a gypsy; Helen and Hero, hildings and harlots; Thisbe, a gray eye or so, but not to the purpose,--

[Enter Romeo.]

Signior Romeo, bon jour! there's a French salutation to your French slop. You gave us the counterfeit fairly last night.

Romeo
Good morrow to you both. What counterfeit did I give you?

Mercutio
The slip, sir, the slip; can you not conceive?

Romeo
Pardon, good Mercutio, my business was great; and in such a case as mine a man may strain courtesy.

Mercutio
That's as much as to say, such a case as yours constrains a man to bow in the hams.

Romeo
Meaning, to court'sy.

Mercutio
Thou hast most kindly hit it.

Romeo
A most courteous exposition.

Mercutio
Nay, I am the very pink of courtesy.

Romeo

Oh, you are a gentleman as fresh as a woman's blooming parts.

Mercutio
Right.

Romeo
Well then, my shoe is decorated with flowers.

Mercutio
Well said. This joke is worn out like the sole of your shoe.

Romeo
You're right. I'm just playing around.

Mercutio
Come on Benvolio. Join us and break up this battle of the wits.

Romeo
If you give up, I'll declare myself the winner, the smartest of us all.

Mercutio
You are on a wild-goose chase, if you are trying to challenge me.

Romeo
You are the goose I'm trying to chase.

Mercutio
I will bite you for saying that.

Romeo
No, good goose, don't bite me.

Pink for flower.

Mercutio
Right.

Romeo
Why, then is my pump well-flowered.

Mercutio
Well said: follow me this jest now till thou hast worn out thy pump;that, when the single sole of it is worn, the jest may remain, after the wearing, sole singular.

Romeo
O single-soled jest, solely singular for the singleness!

Mercutio
Come between us, good Benvolio; my wits faint.

Romeo
Swits and spurs, swits and spurs; or I'll cry a match.

Mercutio
Nay, if thy wits run the wild-goose chase, I have done; for thou hast more of the wild-goose in one of thy wits than, I am sure, I have in my whole five: was I with you there for the goose?

Romeo
Thou wast never with me for anything when thou wast not there for the goose.

Mercutio
I will bite thee by the ear for that jest.

Romeo
Nay, good goose, bite not.

Mercutio
You think you are so smart!

Romeo
Well, that is good for you, since you are a goose.

Mercutio
Ha-ha-ha! Your jokes are spreading a little thin.

Romeo
I have to spread them thinly, word for word, for those who aren't as smart as me.

Mercutio
I prefer this joking over your previous groaning for love. Aren't you more sociable now? You are more like your old self. Love made you a babbling idiot.

Benvolio
Stop there. Stop there.

Mercutio
You want me to stop telling my story. I have only just begun.

Benvolio
That's what I'm afraid of, a long story.

Mercutio
You're wrong, this time. I would have made it short.

Mercutio
Thy wit is a very bitter sweeting; it is a most sharp sauce.

Romeo
And is it not, then, well served in to a sweet goose?

Mercutio
O, here's a wit of cheveril, that stretches from an inch narrow to an ell broad!

Romeo
I stretch it out for that word broad: which added to the goose, proves thee far and wide a broad goose.

Mercutio
Why, is not this better now than groaning for love? now art thou sociable, now art thou Romeo; not art thou what thou art, by art as well as by nature: for this drivelling love is like a great natural, that runs lolling up and down to hide his bauble in a hole.

Benvolio
Stop there, stop there.

Mercutio
Thou desirest me to stop in my tale against the hair.

Benvolio
Thou wouldst else have made thy tale large.

Mercutio
O, thou art deceived; I would have made it short: for I was come to the whole depth of my tale; and meant indeed to occupy the argument no longer.

Romeo Here comes something good. (Enter Nurse and Peter.) **Mercutio** It looks like a ship's sail is coming. **Benvolio** No, it looks like a man and a woman. **Nurse** Peter! **Peter** Here I am. **Nurse** Give me my fan. **Mercutio** Please, Peter, give her the fan to hide her face, because the fan is much better looking. **Nurse** Good morning, gentleman. **Mercutio** Good afternoon, gentlewoman. **Nurse** Is it afternoon already? **Mercutio** Yes, it is. The great hand of the clock is now upon his prick at twelve. **Nurse** You are a disgusting man. Get out of here. **Romeo** My dear woman, made by God, only He	**Romeo** Here's goodly gear! [Enter Nurse and Peter.] **Mercutio** A sail, a sail, a sail! **Benvolio** Two, two; a shirt and a smock. **Nurse** Peter! **Peter** Anon. **Nurse** My fan, Peter. **Mercutio** Good Peter, to hide her face; for her fan's the fairer face. **Nurse** God ye good morrow, gentlemen. **Mercutio** God ye good-den, fair gentlewoman. **Nurse** Is it good-den? **Mercutio** 'Tis no less, I tell ye; for the bawdy hand of the dial is now upon the prick of noon. **Nurse** Out upon you! what a man are you! **Romeo** One, gentlewoman, that God hath made

can destroy you.

Nurse
At least you are honest. Can anyone tell me where is young Romeo?

Romeo
I can tell you, but young Romeo will be older when you find him than he was when you started looking him. I am the youngest person who goes by that name.

Nurse
Don't you speak well?

Mercutio
And he is wise.

Nurse
If you are the Romeo I'm looking for, I need to speak with you in private.

Benvolio
She will probably "indite" him to supper.

Mercutio
Perhaps Romeo is her pimp. I have found him out.

Romeo
What have you found out?

Mercutio
She can't be a prostitute. She's too ugly.

(Sings.)

Hairy Rabbit, hairy rabbit,
Is good meat to eat during Lent.
But if it gets too old,

for himself to mar.

Nurse
By my troth, it is well said;--for himself to mar, quoth 'a?--Gentlemen, can any of you tell me where I may find the young Romeo?

Romeo
I can tell you: but young Romeo will be older when you have found him than he was when you sought him: I am the youngest of that name, for fault of a worse.

Nurse
You say well.

Mercutio
Yea, is the worst well? very well took, i' faith; wisely, wisely.

Nurse
If you be he, sir, I desire some confidence with you.

Benvolio
She will indite him to some supper.

Mercutio
A bawd, a bawd, a bawd! So ho!

Romeo
What hast thou found?

Mercutio
No hare, sir; unless a hare, sir, in a lenten pie, that is something stale and hoar ere it be spent. [Sings.] An old hare hoar, And an old hare hoar, Is very good meat in Lent; But a hare that is hoar Is too much for a score When it hoars ere it be spent.

Your money is already spent.
Hey Romeo, are you going to your
father's house for lunch?

Romeo
Yes, you go ahead. I'll be right behind
you.

Mercutio
Farewell, old lady. Farewell.

(Singing.)

Lady, lady, lady.

(Exit Mercutio and Benvolio.)

Nurse
Good Lord! Who was that crazy fellow,
so full of himself?

Romeo
He is a gentleman, Nurse. He just loves
to hear himself talk and boy, can he talk!

Nurse
If he says anything against me, I'll kick
his butt. And, if I can't do it, I'll find
someone who can. I am not one of his
buddies or slutty girlfriends. And you,
Peter, you just stood by and let him talk to
me that way.

Peter
I didn't see any harm in him. If I had, I
would surely have come to your defense.
I promise you, I am as quick as any man
to defend a lady.

Romeo, will you come to your father's?
we'll to dinner thither.

Romeo
I will follow you.

Mercutio
Farewell, ancient lady; farewell,--
[singing] lady, lady, lady.

 [Exeunt Mercutio, and Benvolio.]

Nurse
Marry, farewell!--I pray you, sir, what
saucy merchant was this that was so full
of his ropery?

Romeo
A gentleman, nurse, that loves to hear
himself talk; and will speak more in a
minute than he will stand to in a month.

Nurse
An 'a speak anything against me, I'll take
him down, an'a were lustier than he is,
and twenty such Jacks; and if I cannot, I'll
find those that shall. Scurvy knave! I am
none of his flirt-gills; I am none of his
skains-mates.--And thou must stand by
too, and suffer every knave to use me at
his pleasure!

Peter
I saw no man use you at his pleasure; if I
had, my weapon should quickly have been
out, I warrant you: I dare draw as soon as
another man, if I see occasion in a good
quarrel, and the law on my side.

Nurse
I swear! I am so angry that I am shaking all over. Romeo, I still need to have a word with you. My young lady asked me to find you and what she said I will keep to myself if you tend to hurt her in any way. Remember she is young and naïve when it comes to love.

Romeo
Nurse, I promise you I…

Nurse
I think you have a good heart, sir, and I will tell her. Lord, she will be a happy girl.

Romeo
What are you going to tell her? You won't let me finish what I have to say.

Nurse
I'll tell her that you propose marriage to her, the gentlemanly thing to do.

Romeo
Tell her to find some way to come to the abbey this afternoon. By Friar Lawrence, we will confess our sins and be married. (Giving her money.) Please take this for your trouble.

Nurse
I can't take your money.

Romeo

Nurse
Now, afore God, I am so vexed that every part about me quivers. Scurvy knave!-- Pray you, sir, a word: and, as I told you, my young lady bid me enquire you out; what she bade me say I will keep to myself: but first let me tell ye, if ye should lead her into a fool's paradise, as they say, it were a very gross kind of behaviour, as they say: for the gentlewoman is young; and, therefore, if you should deal double with her, truly it were an ill thing to be offered to any gentlewoman, and very weak dealing.

Romeo
Nurse, commend me to thy lady and mistress. I protest unto thee,--

Nurse
Good heart, and i' faith I will tell her as much: Lord, Lord, she will be a joyful woman.

Romeo
What wilt thou tell her, nurse? thou dost not mark me.

Nurse
I will tell her, sir,--that you do protest: which, as I take it, is a gentlemanlike offer.

Romeo
Bid her devise some means to come to shrift This afternoon; And there she shall at Friar Lawrence' cell Be shriv'd and married. Here is for thy pains.

Nurse
No, truly, sir; not a penny.

Romeo

But, I insist.

Nurse
(Taking the money.) You said this afternoon, right? She will be there.

Romeo
Wait, good Nurse. I'll send someone within an hour to meet you behind the abbey wall. He will bring a rope so I may meet Juliet secretly. Goodbye now and I will pay you for your help. Don't forget to talk me up to Juliet.

Nurse
God bless you. And, one more thing…

Romeo
What did you say?

Nurse
Are you sure you can trust the man you are sending? You know what they say about keeping secrets.

Romeo
I promise you. I trust him.

Nurse
My mistress is the sweetest lady. When she was just little thing--There is a man in town who also wants her by the name of Paris. I told her he would make a better husband than you, but she would rather marry a toad as to marry him. Doesn't rosemary and Romeo start with the same letter?

Go to; I say you shall.

Nurse
This afternoon, sir? well, she shall be there.

Romeo
And stay, good nurse, behind the abbey-wall: Within this hour my man shall be with thee, And bring thee cords made like a tackled stair; Which to the high top-gallant of my joy Must be my convoy in the secret night. Farewell; be trusty, and I'll quit thy pains: Farewell; commend me to thy mistress.

Nurse
Now God in heaven bless thee!--Hark you, sir.

Romeo
What say'st thou, my dear nurse?

Nurse
Is your man secret? Did you ne'er hear say, Two may keep counsel, putting one away?

Romeo
I warrant thee, my man's as true as steel.

Nurse
Well, sir; my mistress is the sweetest lady.--Lord, Lord! when 'twas a little prating thing,--O, there's a nobleman in town, one Paris, that would fain lay knife aboard; but she, good soul, had as lief see a toad, a very toad, as see him. I anger her sometimes, and tell her that Paris is the properer man; but I'll warrant you, when I say so, she looks as pale as any clout in the versal world. Doth not rosemary and Romeo begin both with a letter?

Romeo Yes ma'am. They both begin with 'r'.	**Romeo** Ay, nurse; what of that? both with an R.
Nurse You are so silly. 'R' is for the name of a dog. They must begin with a different letter. You should hear Juliet talk about you and rosemary.	**Nurse** Ah, mocker! that's the dog's name. R is for the dog: no; I know it begins with some other letter:--and she hath the prettiest sententious of it, of you and rosemary, that it would do you good to hear it.
Romeo Okay, please send my message to your lady.	**Romeo** Commend me to thy lady.
Nurse Certainly, a thousand times, I will. (Exit Romeo.) Peter!	**Nurse** Ay, a thousand times. [Exit Romeo.]--Peter!
Peter Yes?	**Peter** Anon?
Nurse Peter, take my fan, and go ahead.	**Nurse** Peter, take my fan, and go before.
(Exit all.)	[Exeunt.]

Scene V: Capulet's garden.

(Enter Juliet.)

Juliet I sent the nurse at nine o'clock. She promised to return in thirty minutes. Perhaps, she cannot find him. She is so inept! Love's messengers should be as fast as thoughts, like sunbeams, moving shadows or the wings of a dove. Now it's noon. Three hours have passed. Still, she is not here. Maybe if she were younger, she would be faster, inspired by my words of love and my love's to me. But old folks act as if they were dead, slow and heavy as lead. Oh God, here she comes! (Enter Nurse and Peter.) Oh sweet Nurse, what did you find out? Did you find Romeo? Send your man away.	**Juliet** The clock struck nine when I did send the nurse; In half an hour she promis'd to return. Perchance she cannot meet him: that's not so.-- O, she is lame! love's heralds should be thoughts, Which ten times faster glide than the sun's beams, Driving back shadows over lowering hills: Therefore do nimble-pinion'd doves draw love, And therefore hath the wind-swift Cupid wings. Now is the sun upon the highmost hill Of this day's journey; and from nine till twelve Is three long hours,-- yet she is not come. Had she affections and warm youthful blood, She'd be as swift in motion as a ball; My words would bandy her to my sweet love, And his to me: But old folks, many feign as they were dead; Unwieldy, slow, heavy and pale as lead.-- O God, she comes! [Enter Nurse and Peter]. O honey nurse, what news? Hast thou met with him? Send thy man away.
Nurse Stay at the gate. (Exit Peter.)	**Nurse** Peter, stay at the gate. [Exit Peter.]
Juliet Why do you look so sad? If it's bad news, break it to me gently. If it's good news, then why do you come in here with such a sour face?	**Juliet** Now, good sweet nurse,--O Lord, why look'st thou sad? Though news be sad, yet tell them merrily; If good, thou sham'st the music of sweet news By playing it to me with so sour a face.
Nurse	**Nurse**

I am weary. Just give me a minute. My bones ache and I have had quite a journey!

Juliet
I would give you my bones for some news. Please, I beg you, speak. Good, good Nurse, tell me.

Nurse
You're in a hurry. Can't you wait a minute? Don't you see I am out of breath?

Juliet
You can't be out of breath, if you can say you're out of breath. You could have told me by now. Is it good or bad news? Can you answer that? Just tell me one way or the other, and then I'll be patient. Give me something, good or bad.

Nurse
I think you have made a bad choice with Romeo. You don't know how to pick a man. Yes, his face is handsome and his legs are great, but the rest of his body isn't much. He is not courteous, but I think he is gentle. But it is your choice. Remember to serve God. Have you had lunch yet?

Juliet
No, I haven't eaten and I already knew all of this. What did he say about our marriage?

Nurse
Lord, my head hurts. It feels like it is

I am aweary, give me leave awhile;-- Fie, how my bones ache! what a jaunt have I had!

Juliet
I would thou hadst my bones, and I thy news: Nay, come, I pray thee speak;-- good, good nurse, speak.

Nurse
Jesu, what haste? can you not stay awhile? Do you not see that I am out of breath?

Juliet
How art thou out of breath, when thou hast breath To say to me that thou art out of breath? The excuse that thou dost make in this delay Is longer than the tale thou dost excuse. Is thy news good or bad? answer to that; Say either, and I'll stay the circumstance: Let me be satisfied, is't good or bad?

Nurse
Well, you have made a simple choice; you know not how to choose a man: Romeo! no, not he; rhough his face be better than any man's, yet his leg excels all men's; and for a hand and a foot, and a body,--though they be not to be talked on, yet they are past compare: he is not the flower of courtesy,--but I'll warrant him as gentle as a lamb.--Go thy ways, wench; serve God.--What, have you dined at home?

Juliet
No, no: but all this did I know before. What says he of our marriage? what of that?

Nurse
Lord, how my head aches! what a head

about to burst into twenty pieces. My back is killing me, too! How could you send me on a trip like this knowing what it would do to me?

Juliet
I am sorry that you are not feeling well. Sweet, sweet, sweet Nurse, tell me what he said.

Nurse
He says, like an honest, polite, kind, and handsome man, and I bet a virtuous one, too…Where is your mother?

Juliet
Where is my mother? She is inside. Where else would she be? Quit being so vague.

Nurse
Why are you so angry? Is this how you treat your helper? From now on, you can do your own dirty work.

Juliet
Quit being so fussy. What did Romeo say?

Nurse
Have you figured out how to get to the church today?

Juliet
Yes.

Nurse
Then, go to Friar Lawrence for the ceremony. Romeo will meet you there. Here comes the blood to your cheeks.

have I! It beats as it would fall in twenty pieces. My back o' t' other side,--O, my back, my back!-- Beshrew your heart for sending me about To catch my death with jauncing up and down!

Juliet
I' faith, I am sorry that thou art not well. Sweet, sweet, sweet nurse, tell me, what says my love?

Nurse
Your love says, like an honest gentleman, And a courteous, and a kind, and a handsome; And, I warrant, a virtuous,-- Where is your mother?

Juliet
Where is my mother?--why, she is within; Where should she be? How oddly thou repliest! 'Your love says, like an honest gentleman,-- 'Where is your mother?'

Nurse
O God's lady dear! Are you so hot? marry,come up, I trow; Is this the poultice for my aching bones? Henceforward,do your messages yourself.

Juliet
Here's such a coil!--come, what says Romeo?

Nurse
Have you got leave to go to shrift to-day?

Juliet
I have.

Nurse
Then hie you hence to Friar Lawrence' cell; There stays a husband to make you a wife: Now comes the wanton blood up in

While you go to church, I have to get a ladder from your love so he can come to you after dark. I must do all the work while you get all of the rewards, especially tonight. Go on now. I am going to eat.

Juliet
Thank you, dear Nurse. Wish me luck!

(Exit all.)

your cheeks, They'll be in scarlet straight at any news. Hie you to church; I must another way, To fetch a ladder, by the which your love Must climb a bird's nest soon when it is dark: I am the drudge, and toil in your delight; But you shall bear the burden soon at night. Go; I'll to dinner; hie you to the cell.

Juliet
Hie to high fortune!--honest nurse, farewell.

[Exeunt.]

Scene VI: Friar Lawrence's Cell.

(Enter Friar Lawrence and Romeo.)

Friar Lawrence
The heavens smile down upon the act of marriage. I hope we are not sorry afterwards.

Friar
So smile the heavens upon this holy act
That after-hours with sorrow chide us not!

Romeo
Amen. No matter what happens, nothing can change the joy I feel when I see my love. Just marry us, and let death do us part. It's enough that I can call her mine.

Romeo
Amen, amen! but come what sorrow can, It cannot countervail the exchange of joy That one short minute gives me in her sight: Do thou but close our hands with holy words, Then love-devouring death do what he dare,-- It is enough I may but call her mine.

Friar Lawrence
Sometimes acts that give us great pleasure bring us great sadness. They quickly ignite and as quickly extinguish. Like honey, too much of a sweet thing can make one sick. Therefore, don't love each other too much. This is the key to a relationship that lasts. Being too passionate can be as bad as loving too slowly. Here comes your lady, now. She is so light on her feet, like she is floating on air. Ah, love.

Friar
These violent delights have violent ends, And in their triumph die; like fire and powder, Which, as they kiss, consume: the sweetest honey Is loathsome in his own deliciousness, And in the taste confounds the appetite: Therefore love moderately: long love doth so; Too swift arrives as tardy as too slow. Here comes the lady:-- O, so light a foot Will ne'er wear out the everlasting flint: A lover may bestride the gossamer That idles in the wanton summer air And yet not fall; so light is vanity.

(Enter Juliet.)

[Enter Juliet.]

Juliet
Good evening, my father.

Juliet
Good-even to my ghostly confessor.

Friar Lawrence
Romeo will thank you for both of us.

Friar
Romeo shall thank thee, daughter, for us both.

Juliet
Then, I will thank him.

Romeo
Ah Juliet, are you as happy as I am? If you are, tell me how you feel about our future.

Juliet
I can't quite put it into words. I can only say that I am filled with a wealth of blessings and happiness.

Friar Lawrence
Come on. Let's go. This will not take long, and since we are in church, I am not leaving you two alone until you are married.

(Exit all.)

Juliet
As much to him, else is his thanks too much.

Romeo
Ah, Juliet, if the measure of thy joy Be heap'd like mine, and that thy skill be more To blazon it, then sweeten with thy breath This neighbour air, and let rich music's tongue Unfold the imagin'd happiness that both Receive in either by this dear encounter.

Juliet
Conceit, more rich in matter than in words, Brags of his substance, not of ornament: They are but beggars that can count their worth; But my true love is grown to such excess, I cannot sum up sum of half my wealth.

Friar
Come, come with me, and we will make short work; For, by your leaves, you shall not stay alone Till holy church incorporate two in one.

[Exeunt.]

Act III

Scene I: A public place.

(Enter Mercutio, Benvolio, Page, and Servants.)

Benvolio
I beg you, Mercutio, let's go home. It is too hot. The Capulets are out, too, and I don't feel like fighting. You know how hot days make people irritable.

Mercutio
You are like one of those guys who go into a bar with a weapon, but say he doesn't want to use it. After a couple of drinks, you pull it out on someone for no reason.

Benvolio
You think I am like that?

Mercutio
You know you are as hot-headed as any other man in Italy. It doesn't take much to get you in a bad mood, and when you are in a bad mood, it doesn't take much to make you angry.

Benvolio
Angry, about what?

Mercutio
If there were two Benvolios in the world, they would fight each other to the death. You would fight with a man over how many hairs are in his beard. You would fight a man for cracking nuts, the same color as your eyes. Who else would fight over such stupid things? Your head is as

Benvolio
I pray thee, good Mercutio, let's retire:
The day is hot, the Capulets abroad, And, if we meet, we shall not scape a brawl;
For now, these hot days, is the mad blood stirring.

Mercutio
Thou art like one of these fellows that, when he enters the confines of a tavern, claps me his sword upon the table, and says 'God send me no need of thee!' and by the operation of the second cup draws him on the drawer, when indeed there is no need.

Benvolio
Am I like such a fellow?

Mercutio
Come, come, thou art as hot a Jack in thy mood as any in Italy; and as soon moved to be moody, and as soon moody to be moved.

Benvolio
And what to?

Mercutio
Nay, an there were two such, we should have none shortly, for one would kill the other. Thou! why, thou wilt quarrel with a man that hath a hair more or a hair less in his beard than thou hast. Thou wilt quarrel with a man for cracking nuts, having no other reason but because thou hast hazel

full of reasons to fight as an egg is full of yolks. Your mind is like scrambled eggs, you have been in so many fights. You have fought because a man, coughing in the street, woke up your dog. Didn't you even fight with a tailor for wearing a summer suit before Easter? And another, for tying new shoes with old laces? Now, you stand there and scold me about fighting!

Benvolio
If I fought as much as you, I couldn't afford simple life insurance.

Mercutio
Simple life insurance? You're simple-minded.

Benvolio
What now? Here comes the Capulets.

Mercutio
Let them. I don't care.

(Enter Tybalt and others.)

Tybalt
Stay close, guys. I will speak to them. Gentlemen, good afternoon. May I have a word with one of you?

Mercutio
Just one word with one of us? I think you would like to have a word and something else. Blow off.

Tybalt
I could do that, if you give me a reason.

eyes;--what eye but such an eye would spy out such a quarrel? Thy head is as full of quarrels as an egg is full of meat; and yet thy head hath been beaten as addle as an egg for quarrelling. Thou hast quarrelled with a man for coughing in the street, because he hath wakened thy dog that hath lain asleep in the sun. Didst thou not fall out with a tailor for wearing his new doublet before Easter? with another for tying his new shoes with an old riband? and yet thou wilt tutor me from quarrelling!

Benvolio
An I were so apt to quarrel as thou art, any man should buy the fee simple of my life for an hour and a quarter.

Mercutio
The fee simple! O simple!

Benvolio
By my head, here come the Capulets.

Mercutio
By my heel, I care not.

[Enter Tybalt and others.]

Tybalt
Follow me close, for I will speak to them.--Gentlemen, good-den: a word with one of you.

Mercutio
And but one word with one of us? Couple it with something; make it a word and a blow.

Tybalt
You shall find me apt enough to that, sir, an you will give me occasion.

Mercutio
You can't find a reason on your own?

Tybalt
You are a friend of Romeo's, right?

Mercutio
A friend! Do you think we are a band? If so, here is my drumstick (referring to his sword) and I can make you dance with it. Friends!

Benvolio
Not here in public. There are too many eyes. Either we go somewhere private to hash this out, or just leave it alone.

Mercutio
I don't care if we're in public. Let people look. I am not going anywhere to please anyone.

Tybalt
I have no fight with you. Here comes my man.

(Enter Romeo.)

Mercutio
I'll be damned if he's your man. Unless you run and he chases you, you can't call him your man.

Tybalt
Romeo, I have a word for you. You are a villain.

Romeo
Tybalt, you have no reason to greet me

Mercutio
Could you not take some occasion without giving?

Tybalt
Mercutio, thou consortest with Romeo,--

Mercutio
Consort! what, dost thou make us minstrels? An thou make minstrels of us, look to hear nothing but discords: here's my fiddlestick; here's that shall make you dance. Zounds, consort!

Benvolio
We talk here in the public haunt of men: Either withdraw unto some private place, And reason coldly of your grievances, Or else depart; here all eyes gaze on us.

Mercutio
Men's eyes were made to look, and let them gaze; I will not budge for no man's pleasure, I.

Tybalt
Well, peace be with you, sir.--Here comes my man.

[Enter Romeo.]

Mercutio
But I'll be hanged, sir, if he wear your livery: Marry, go before to field, he'll be your follower; Your worship in that sense may call him man.

Tybalt
Romeo, the love I bear thee can afford No better term than this,--Thou art a villain.

Romeo
Tybalt, the reason that I have to love thee

that way. I love you and have no feelings of rage against you. I am no villain, so leave me alone. Things have changed. You don't know me very well.

Tybalt
You may not have rage, but I do. There is no excuse for the way you have treated me. Now get ready to fight.

Romeo
I'm not fighting you. I would never hurt you. You should know that I have my reasons and they are filled with love. So, Capulet, a name I love like my own, just stop.

Mercutio
Oh Romeo, you wimp. You make me sick. (Draws sword.) Tybalt, you rat-catcher, are you just going to walk away?

Tybalt
What do you want?

Mercutio
You, pussy! I just want one of your nine lives, or I might beat the other eight out of you. Draw your sword, or I am going to take one of your ears.

Tybalt
I'll give you a fight if that's what you want. (Draws his sword.)

Romeo
Mercutio, put your sword away.

Mercutio
Come on, sir. Give me your best shot.

Doth much excuse the appertaining rage To such a greeting. Villain am I none; Therefore farewell; I see thou know'st me not.

Tybalt
Boy, this shall not excuse the injuries That thou hast done me; therefore turn and draw.

Romeo
I do protest I never injur'd thee; But love thee better than thou canst devise Till thou shalt know the reason of my love: And so good Capulet,--which name I tender As dearly as mine own,--be satisfied.

Mercutio
O calm, dishonourable, vile submission! Alla stoccata carries it away. [Draws.] Tybalt, you rat-catcher, will you walk?

Tybalt
What wouldst thou have with me?

Mercutio
Good king of cats, nothing but one of your nine lives; that I mean to make bold withal, and, as you shall use me hereafter, dry-beat the rest of the eight. Will you pluck your sword out of his pitcher by the ears? make haste, lest mine be about your ears ere it be out.

Tybalt
I am for you. [Drawing.]

Romeo
Gentle Mercutio, put thy rapier up.

Mercutio
Come, sir, your passado.

(They fight.)	[They fight.]

Romeo

Help, Benvolio! Draw your sword!
(Trying to break them up.) Gentlemen,
this is crazy! Stop this outrage! The
prince has forbidden fighting in the
streets. Stop, Tybalt! Mercutio!

(Exit Tybalt and others.)

Mercutio

I am hurt. Curse both of you. I am dying.
Did Tybalt walk away uninjured?

Benvolio

Are you hurt?

Mercutio

A scratch, only a scratch, but it is enough.
Where is my boy? (To the page.) Go,
fool, get me a doctor.

(Exit Page.)

Romeo

Be brave. You can't be hurt that bad.

Mercutio

It's not quite as deep as a well or wide as
a church door, but it is enough. If you ask
for me tomorrow, I will be in my grave. I
am dying. Curse the Montagues and the
Capulets. I can't believe that dog, that rat,
that mouse, that cat could scratch me to
death. He learned his swordsmanship
from a book. Why did you try to stop us?
This is your fault.

Romeo

Romeo

Draw, Benvolio; beat down their
weapons.-- Gentlemen, for shame! forbear
this outrage!-- Tybalt,--Mercutio,--the
prince expressly hath Forbid this
bandying in Verona streets.-- Hold,
Tybalt!--good Mercutio!-- [Exeunt Tybalt
with his Partizans.]

Mercutio

I am hurt;-- A plague o' both your
houses!--I am sped.-- Is he gone, and hath
nothing?

Benvolio

What, art thou hurt?

Mercutio

Ay, ay, a scratch, a scratch; marry, 'tis
enough.-- Where is my page?--go, villain,
fetch a surgeon.

[Exit Page.]

Romeo

Courage, man; the hurt cannot be much.

Mercutio

No, 'tis not so deep as a well, nor so wide
as a church door; but 'tis enough, 'twill
serve: ask for me to-morrow, and you
shall find me a grave man. I am peppered,
I warrant, for this world.--A plague o'
both your houses!--Zounds, a dog, a rat, a
mouse, a cat, to scratch a man to death! a
braggart, a rogue, a villain, that fights by
the book of arithmetic!--Why the devil
came you between us? I was hurt under
your arm.

Romeo

I didn't want you to get hurt.

Mercutio
Help me into a house, Benvolio. I feel faint. Curse you, Romeo, and Tybalt, too. You have made worms' food out of me.

(Exit Mercutio and Benvolio.)

Romeo
Mercutio, the prince's relative and my friend, has been killed because of me. He was trying to protect me from Tybalt, who has been my cousin for only an hour. Oh Juliet, your beauty has made me soft where I once was hard as steel.

(Enter Benvolio.)

Benvolio
Romeo, Romeo. Brave Mercutio is dead. His courageous spirit has ascended into the clouds. He was too young to die.

Romeo
This black day is only the beginning. Today is the start of new trouble and the end is ahead.

Benvolio
Here comes Tybalt, again.

Romeo
Have you come to gloat in triumph? Mercutio is dead! You belong in heaven and I aim to put you there. Call me a villain, again. Mercutio is waiting for you or me or both of us.

I thought all for the best.

Mercutio
Help me into some house, Benvolio, Or I shall faint.--A plague o' both your houses! They have made worms' meat of me: I have it, and soundly too.--Your houses!

[Exit Mercutio and Benvolio.]

Romeo
This gentleman, the prince's near ally, My very friend, hath got his mortal hurt In my behalf; my reputation stain'd With Tybalt's slander,--Tybalt, that an hour Hath been my kinsman.--O sweet Juliet, Thy beauty hath made me effeminate And in my temper soften'd valour's steel.

[Re-enter Benvolio.]

Benvolio
O Romeo, Romeo, brave Mercutio's dead! That gallant spirit hath aspir'd the clouds, Which too untimely here did scorn the earth.

Romeo
This day's black fate on more days doth depend; This but begins the woe others must end.

Benvolio
Here comes the furious Tybalt back again.

Romeo
Alive in triumph! and Mercutio slain! Away to heaven respective lenity, And fire-ey'd fury be my conduct now!--

[Re-enter Tybalt.]

Now, Tybalt, take the 'villain' back again That late thou gavest me; for Mercutio's

Tybalt
You wretched boy. You will be with him soon.

Romeo
We'll see about that.

(They fight.)

Benvolio
Get out of here, Romeo! You have killed Tybalt and people are coming. Shake out of it. The prince will execute you if he finds you. Get out of here!

Romeo
I am the biggest fool. My future is over!

Benvolio
Why are you still here?

(Exit Romeo.)

(Enter Citizens.)

Citizens
Which way did Mercutio's murderer go? Which way did Tybalt go?

Benvolio
Tybalt is lying over there.

Citizens
Get up, sir, and go with me. In the name of the Prince, I command you to obey my orders.

(Enter Prince, Montague, Capulet, their wives, and others.)

---

soul Is but a little way above our heads, Staying for thine to keep him company. Either thou or I, or both, must go with him.

Tybalt
Thou, wretched boy, that didst consort him here, Shalt with him hence.

Romeo
This shall determine that.

[They fight; Tybalt falls.]

Benvolio
Romeo, away, be gone! The citizens are up, and Tybalt slain.-- Stand not amaz'd. The prince will doom thee death If thou art taken. Hence, be gone, away!

Romeo
O, I am fortune's fool!

Benvolio
Why dost thou stay?

[Exit Romeo.]

[Enter Citizens, &c.]

1 Citizen
Which way ran he that kill'd Mercutio? Tybalt, that murderer, which way ran he?

Benvolio
There lies that Tybalt.

1 Citizen
Up, sir, go with me; I charge thee in the prince's name obey.

[Enter Prince, attended; Montague, Capulet, their Wives, and others.]

Prince
Where are the villains who started all of this?

Benvolio
I can tell you everyone who was involved. There lays the man killed by Romeo, who killed his friend, Mercutio.

Lady Capulet
My cousin, Tybalt? Oh no, my brother's child! Oh, Prince! Husband! Oh, my poor cousin is dead! Prince, you must avenge his death with the death of a Montague. Oh, cousin, cousin!

Prince
Benvolio, who started all of this?

Benvolio
Tybalt started it. Romeo tried to speak with him and calm him down. He got down on his knees to try and reason with him, but Tybalt would not let up. Romeo tried to break them up, but Tybalt got around him and stabbed Mercutio. Then, he ran. When Tybalt came back, Romeo was so angry he killed him. I tried to stop them, but it all happened so fast. Then, Romeo fled. This is the truth. I swear it on my life.

Prince
Where are the vile beginners of this fray?

Benvolio
O noble prince. I can discover all The unlucky manage of this fatal brawl: There lies the man, slain by young Romeo, That slew thy kinsman, brave Mercutio.

Lady Capulet
Tybalt, my cousin! O my brother's child!-- O prince!--O husband!--O, the blood is spill'd Of my dear kinsman!--Prince, as thou art true, For blood of ours shed blood of Montague.-- O cousin, cousin!

Prince
Benvolio, who began this bloody fray?

Benvolio
Tybalt, here slain, whom Romeo's hand did slay; Romeo, that spoke him fair, bid him bethink How nice the quarrel was, and urg'd withal Your high displeasure.-- All this,--uttered With gentle breath, calm look, knees humbly bow'd,-- Could not take truce with the unruly spleen Of Tybalt, deaf to peace, but that he tilts With piercing steel at bold Mercutio's breast; Who, all as hot, turns deadly point to point, And, with a martial scorn, with one hand beats Cold death aside, and with the other sends It back to Tybalt, whose dexterity Retorts it: Romeo he cries aloud, 'Hold, friends! friends, part!' and swifter than his tongue, His agile arm beats down their fatal points, And 'twixt them rushes; underneath whose arm An envious thrust from Tybalt hit the life Of stout Mercutio, and then Tybalt fled: But by-and-by comes back to Romeo, Who had but newly entertain'd revenge, And to't they

Lady Capulet
He is lying. He is related to the Montagues. It would take at least twenty of them to take Tybalt down. Now, I beg for justice, Prince. Romeo killed Tybalt, so he must not live.

Prince
Romeo killed Tybalt, who killed Mercutio. So, who will you have me kill, next?

Montague
Not Romeo, Prince. He was Mercutio's friend. He was only following the law, an eye for an eye.

Prince
And for that, we will exile him. Remember, Mercutio was my relative, too, and I will heap fines so heavy upon both of you that you will wish this feud had never begun. I will not listen to any more of your pleading and excuses, or your tears and prayers. Therefore, Romeo may live in exile. If he is found, he will be executed. Take away this body and listen to what I say. Showing mercy to murderers only means more bloodshed.

(Exit all.)

go like lightning; for, ere I Could draw to part them was stout Tybalt slain; And as he fell did Romeo turn and fly. This is the truth, or let Benvolio die.

Lady Capulet
He is a kinsman to the Montague, Affection makes him false, he speaks not true: Some twenty of them fought in this black strife, And all those twenty could but kill one life. I beg for justice, which thou, prince, must give; Romeo slew Tybalt, Romeo must not live.

Prince
Romeo slew him; he slew Mercutio: Who now the price of his dear blood doth owe?

Montague
Not Romeo, prince; he was Mercutio's friend; His fault concludes but what the law should end, The life of Tybalt.

Prince
And for that offence Immediately we do exile him hence: I have an interest in your hate's proceeding, My blood for your rude brawls doth lie a-bleeding; But I'll amerce you with so strong a fine That you shall all repent the loss of mine: I will be deaf to pleading and excuses; Nor tears nor prayers shall purchase out abuses, Therefore use none: let Romeo hence in haste, Else, when he is found, that hour is his last. Bear hence this body, and attend our will: Mercy but murders, pardoning those that kill.

[Exeunt.]

Scene II: A room in Capulet's house.

(Enter Juliet.)

Juliet	**Juliet**
Hurry up sun and set already. Come on cloudy night, bring my love to me. They say love is blind, and so what a perfect time for lovers to be together. Come on black night, so I may give myself to Romeo. Come on night. Come on Romeo. You brighten the night like freshly fallen snow on the wings of a raven. Come on night, gentle, loving night. Bring me my Romeo and when he dies, turn him into stars to decorate the face of heaven. Then, everyone will be in love with night, and forget about the sun. Even though I am married, I have not performed my wifely duties. I have not enjoyed my husband. I feel like a child, with new clothes on the night before a festival, unable to wear them. Here comes my nurse. I bet she has news. Everyone who says the name, Romeo, sounds angelic. (Enter Nurse.) What news do you have, Nurse? Is that the rope ladder for Romeo?	Gallop apace, you fiery-footed steeds, Towards Phoebus' lodging; such a waggoner As Phaeton would whip you to the west And bring in cloudy night immediately.-- Spread thy close curtain, love-performing night! That rude eyes may wink, and Romeo Leap to these arms, untalk'd of and unseen.-- Lovers can see to do their amorous rites By their own beauties: or, if love be blind, It best agrees with night.--Come, civil night, Thou sober-suited matron, all in black, And learn me how to lose a winning match, Play'd for a pair of stainless maidenhoods: Hood my unmann'd blood, bating in my cheeks, With thy black mantle; till strange love, grown bold, Think true love acted simple modesty. Come, night;--come, Romeo;--come, thou day in night; For thou wilt lie upon the wings of night Whiter than new snow upon a raven's back.-- Come, gentle night;--come, loving, black-brow'd night, Give me my Romeo; and, when he shall die, Take him and cut him out in little stars, And he will make the face of heaven so fine That all the world will be in love with night, And pay no worship to the garish sun.-- O, I have bought the mansion of a love, But not possess'd it; and, though I am sold, Not yet enjoy'd: so tedious is this day As is the night before some festival To an impatient child that hath new robes, And may not wear them. O, here comes my nurse, And she brings news; and every tongue that speaks But Romeo's name speaks

Nurse
Yes, this is the rope ladder.

(Throws it down.)

Juliet
Well, what is your news? Why do you look so worried?

Nurse
It has been a day! He's dead. He's dead. He's dead! We are in big trouble, lady, big trouble. What an awful day—He's gone, he's killed, and he's dead.

Juliet
Can heaven be so jealous?

Nurse
Romeo can be, but not heaven. Romeo, Romeo! Who would have ever thought him capable of such awfulness?

Juliet
Stop talking like that! It is torture. Has Romeo killed himself? If you say, yes, then I will poison myself. If he is dead, say yes or no. Hurry, and end my worries and decide my fate.

Nurse
I saw the wound with my own eyes. He

heavenly eloquence.--

[Enter Nurse, with cords.]

Now, nurse, what news? What hast thou there? the cords That Romeo bid thee fetch?

Nurse
Ay, ay, the cords.

[Throws them down.]

Juliet
Ah me! what news? why dost thou wring thy hands?

Nurse
Ah, well-a-day! he's dead, he's dead, he's dead! We are undone, lady, we are undone!-- Alack the day!--he's gone, he's kill'd, he's dead!

Juliet
Can heaven be so envious?

Nurse
Romeo can, Though heaven cannot.--O Romeo, Romeo!-- Who ever would have thought it?--Romeo!

Juliet
What devil art thou, that dost torment me thus? This torture should be roar'd in dismal hell. Hath Romeo slain himself? say thou but I, And that bare vowel I shall poison more Than the death-darting eye of cockatrice: I am not I if there be such an I; Or those eyes shut that make thee answer I. If he be slain, say I; or if not, no: Brief sounds determine of my weal or woe.

Nurse
I saw the wound, I saw it with mine eyes,-

was stabbed in the breast and pale from the loss of blood. I saw the gory mess and nearly fainted.

Juliet
Go ahead heart and break. I wish to die or be put in to prison, never to be free again. Put me in the ground with Romeo.

Nurse
Oh, Tybalt. He was the best friend I ever had. Oh polite, honest, Tybalt, I never thought I would live to see your death.

Juliet
What are you talking about? Are Romeo, my husband, and Tybalt, my cousin, both dead? How could something so terrible happen? What is left to live for, if they are gone?

Nurse
Tybalt is gone, and Romeo is banished. Romeo killed Tybalt, and now he is banished.

Juliet
Oh God! Romeo killed Tybalt?

Nurse
Yes, he did, today.

Juliet
He is a snake hiding in the flowers. He is a dragon deep in a beautiful cave. Beautiful tyrant! Angelic fiend! White raven! A predator! He seems so divine, but he is just the opposite. He is like a

- God save the mark!--here on his manly breast. A piteous corse, a bloody piteous corse; Pale, pale as ashes, all bedaub'd in blood, All in gore-blood;--I swounded at the sight.

Juliet
O, break, my heart!--poor bankrout, break at once! To prison, eyes; ne'er look on liberty! Vile earth, to earth resign; end motion here; And thou and Romeo press one heavy bier!

Nurse
O Tybalt, Tybalt, the best friend I had! O courteous Tybalt! honest gentleman! That ever I should live to see thee dead!

Juliet
What storm is this that blows so contrary? Is Romeo slaughter'd, and is Tybalt dead? My dear-lov'd cousin, and my dearer lord?-- Then, dreadful trumpet, sound the general doom! For who is living, if those two are gone?

Nurse
Tybalt is gone, and Romeo banished; Romeo that kill'd him, he is banished.

Juliet
O God!--did Romeo's hand shed Tybalt's blood?

Nurse
It did, it did; alas the day, it did!

Juliet
O serpent heart, hid with a flowering face! Did ever dragon keep so fair a cave? Beautiful tyrant! fiend angelical! Dove-feather'd raven! wolvish-ravening lamb! Despised substance of divinest show! Just

damned saint or cunning villain. Oh nature, how did such a beautiful creature be born with such fiendish ways? Was there ever a book on evil bound in such a beautiful way? I can't believe someone so deceitful could be so gorgeous.

Nurse
You cannot trust men. They are not honest or faithful.   Where's my servant? Give me something to drink. All of this is making me feel old. Shame on Romeo.

Juliet
Hold your tongue. Don't say such a thing. He is not meant for shame and deserves nothing but honor. Why did I let myself get so angry?

Nurse
How can you speak well of your cousin's murderer?

Juliet
Would you rather I speak badly about my husband? My poor husband, how can we clear your name, when your wife of three hours can't stand by you? I'm sure you were only acting in self-defense. I will not cry tears of sadness, but tears of joy, because Romeo is alive. There is still news I want to forget, and that makes me want to die. Romeo is banished. Nothing, not even Tybalt's death, or my mother's and father's deaths, is as bad as that. Romeo is banished. Where is my mother and father, Nurse?

opposite to what thou justly seem'st, A damned saint, an honourable villain!-- O nature, what hadst thou to do in hell When thou didst bower the spirit of a fiend In mortal paradise of such sweet flesh?-- Was ever book containing such vile matter So fairly bound? O, that deceit should dwell In such a gorgeous palace!

Nurse
There's no trust, No faith, no honesty in men; all perjur'd, All forsworn, all naught, all dissemblers.-- Ah, where's my man? Give me some aqua vitae.-- These griefs, these woes, these sorrows make me old. Shame come to Romeo!

Juliet
Blister'd be thy tongue For such a wish! he was not born to shame: Upon his brow shame is asham'd to sit; For 'tis a throne where honour may be crown'd Sole monarch of the universal earth. O, what a beast was I to chide at him!

Nurse
Will you speak well of him that kill'd your cousin?

Juliet
Shall I speak ill of him that is my husband? Ah, poor my lord, what tongue shall smooth thy name, When I, thy three-hours' wife, have mangled it?-- But wherefore, villain, didst thou kill my cousin? That villain cousin would have kill'd my husband: Back, foolish tears, back to your native spring; Your tributary drops belong to woe, Which you, mistaking, offer up to joy. My husband lives, that Tybalt would have slain; And Tybalt's dead, that would have slain my husband: All this is comfort; wherefore weep I, then? Some word there was,

Nurse
Grieving over Tybalt. Would you like to join them? I can take you.

Juliet
Well, they can grieve over him all they want, but my tears are for Romeo. Pick up that rope ladder. We are both useless, now. I am destined to be an old maid. Come on, Nurse, bring that rope ladder with me to my wedding bed, and let death come take me tonight.

Nurse
Go to your room, and I'll find Romeo for you. I know where he is and he'll be here tonight. I'll go to him at Friar Lawrence's house.

worser than Tybalt's death, That murder'd me: I would forget it fain; But O, it presses to my memory Like damned guilty deeds to sinners' minds: 'Tybalt is dead, and Romeo banished.' That 'banished,' that one word 'banished,' Hath slain ten thousand Tybalts. Tybalt's death Was woe enough, if it had ended there: Or, if sour woe delights in fellowship, And needly will be rank'd with other griefs,-- Why follow'd not, when she said Tybalt's dead, Thy father, or thy mother, nay, or both, Which modern lamentation might have mov'd? But with a rear-ward following Tybalt's death, 'Romeo is banished'--to speak that word Is father, mother, Tybalt, Romeo, Juliet, All slain, all dead: 'Romeo is banished,'-- There is no end, no limit, measure, bound, In that word's death; no words can that woe sound.-- Where is my father and my mother, nurse?

Nurse
Weeping and wailing over Tybalt's corse: Will you go to them? I will bring you thither.

Juliet
Wash they his wounds with tears: mine shall be spent, When theirs are dry, for Romeo's banishment. Take up those cords. Poor ropes, you are beguil'd, Both you and I; for Romeo is exil'd: He made you for a highway to my bed; But I, a maid, die maiden-widowed. Come, cords; come, nurse; I'll to my wedding-bed; And death, not Romeo, take my maidenhead!

Nurse
Hie to your chamber. I'll find Romeo To comfort you: I wot well where he is. Hark ye, your Romeo will be here at night: I'll to him; he is hid at Lawrence' cell.

Juliet	**Juliet**
Oh, Nurse, find him! Give him this ring and tell him to come and say his last goodbye. <div align="center">(Exit all.)</div>	O, find him! give this ring to my true knight, And bid him come to take his last farewell. [Exeunt.]

Scene III: Friar Lawrence's house.

(Enter Friar Lawrence.)

Friar Lawrence Come out Romeo. Don't be afraid, even though "tragedy" is in love with you and you are married to "trouble."	**Friar** Romeo, come forth; come forth, thou fearful man. Affliction is enanmour'd of thy parts, And thou art wedded to calamity. [Enter Romeo.]
Romeo Do you have any news? What is the Prince's sentence? What else must I endure?	**Romeo** Father, what news? what is the prince's doom What sorrow craves acquaintance at my hand, That I yet know not?
Friar Lawrence You have spent too much time suffering. I have news from the Prince.	**Friar** Too familiar Is my dear son with such sour company: I bring thee tidings of the prince's doom.
Romeo Is it less than my doom?	**Romeo** What less than doomsday is the prince's doom?
Friar Lawrence Yes, you are not doomed to die, but to be banished.	**Friar** A gentler judgment vanish'd from his lips,-- Not body's death, but body's banishment.
Romeo Banishment, are you kidding? Death is better than banishment. Don't say banishment.	**Romeo** Ha, banishment? be merciful, say death; For exile hath more terror in his look, Much more than death; do not say banishment.
Friar Lawrence You are banished from Verona, but the world is a huge place.	**Friar** Hence from Verona art thou banished: Be patient, for the world is broad and wide.

Romeo

There is no world outside of Verona for me, except for purgatory or hell. So, banishment is death for me. Banishment is like a golden axe cutting off my head.

Friar Lawrence

How dare you talk that way, you rude and thankless boy? The Prince is being kind to you and not holding you to the law. This is mercy, although you refuse to see it.

Romeo

This is not mercy; it is torture. I want to be here with Juliet where I can look at her like every other undeserving creature. Flies are now more honorable than me. Flies can touch her hands and lips, lips that she thinks are sinful even if they touch each other. I cannot; I am banished. I must flee and leave behind my life. Isn't that death? Don't you have a poison, sharp knife or some other deadly weapon you could use to kill me quickly? Banishment will kill me slowly. Banishment is hell that demons howl about. If you are a man of God and my friend, how can you tear me apart with the word, banishment?

Romeo

There is no world without Verona walls, But purgatory, torture, hell itself. Hence-banished is banish'd from the world, And world's exile is death,--then banished Is death mis-term'd: calling death banishment, Thou cutt'st my head off with a golden axe, And smil'st upon the stroke that murders me.

Friar

O deadly sin! O rude unthankfulness! Thy fault our law calls death; but the kind prince, Taking thy part, hath brush'd aside the law, And turn'd that black word death to banishment: This is dear mercy, and thou see'st it not.

Romeo

'Tis torture, and not mercy: heaven is here, Where Juliet lives; and every cat, and dog, And little mouse, every unworthy thing, Live here in heaven, and may look on her; But Romeo may not.--More validity, More honourable state, more courtship lives In carrion flies than Romeo: they may seize On the white wonder of dear Juliet's hand, And steal immortal blessing from her lips; Who, even in pure and vestal modesty, Still blush, as thinking their own kisses sin; But Romeo may not; he is banished,-- This may flies do, when I from this must fly. And sayest thou yet that exile is not death! Hadst thou no poison mix'd, no sharp-ground knife, No sudden mean of death, though ne'er so mean, But banished to kill me; banished? O friar, the damned use that word in hell; Howlings attend it: how hast thou the heart, Being a divine, a ghostly confessor, A sin-absolver, and my friend profess'd, To mangle me with that word banishment?

Friar Lawrence You, madman, listen to me…	**Friar** Thou fond mad man, hear me speak a little,--
Romeo You will speak of banishment again.	**Romeo** O, thou wilt speak again of banishment.
Friar Lawrence I only want to help you.	**Friar** I'll give thee armour to keep off that word; Adversity's sweet milk, philosophy, To comfort thee, though thou art banished.
Romeo Unless you can figure out a way for Juliet and me to be together or a way to reverse the Prince's sentence, don't speak.	**Romeo** Yet banished? Hang up philosophy! Unless philosophy can make a Juliet, Displant a town, reverse a prince's doom, It helps not, it prevails not,--talk no more.
Friar Lawrence Oh, I see. The madman doesn't want to listen.	**Friar** O, then I see that madmen have no ears.
Romeo Why should I listen to someone who cannot understand?	**Romeo** How should they, when that wise men have no eyes?
Friar Lawrence Just hear me out.	**Friar** Let me dispute with thee of thy estate.
Romeo You can't speak of things you know nothing about. If you were in my shoes, just married to Juliet, accused of murdering Tybalt, and now banished, then, I would listen to you as you tore out your hair and prepared for your death. (Knocking within.)	**Romeo** Thou canst not speak of that thou dost not feel: Wert thou as young as I, Juliet thy love, An hour but married, Tybalt murdered, Doting like me, and like me banished, Then mightst thou speak, then mightst thou tear thy hair, And fall upon the ground, as I do now, Taking the measure of an unmade grave. [Knocking within.]
Friar Lawrence Get up. Someone is knocking. Hide!	**Friar** Arise; one knocks. Good Romeo, hide thyself.

Romeo I'm not hiding, unless a fog comes in here and wraps around me. (Knocking.)	**Romeo** Not I; unless the breath of heartsick groans, Mist-like infold me from the search of eyes. [Knocking.]
Friar Lawrence Listen to how they are knocking. Who's there? Get up, Romeo. They will take you. You need to get up so you can stay here. (Knocking.) Hide in my study. Hurry! I'm coming! I'm coming! (Knocking.) Who's knocking so hard on my door? What do you want?	**Friar** Hark, how they knock!--Who's there?--Romeo, arise; Thou wilt be taken.--Stay awhile;--Stand up; [Knocking.] Run to my study.--By-and-by!--God's will! What simpleness is this.--I come, I come! [Knocking.] Who knocks so hard? whence come you? what's your will?
Nurse Let me come in and I'll tell you. I am here from Juliet.	**Nurse** [Within.] Let me come in, and you shall know my errand; I come from Lady Juliet.
Friar Lawrence You are welcome then. (Enter Nurse.)	**Friar** Welcome then. [Enter Nurse.]
Nurse Oh holy friar, where is Romeo?	**Nurse**. O holy friar, O, tell me, holy friar, Where is my lady's lord, where's Romeo?
Friar Lawrence He is lying over there, in a terrible state of mind.	**Friar** There on the ground, with his own tears made drunk.
Nurse Just like my Juliet.	**Nurse** O, he is even in my mistress' case,-- Just in her case!

Friar Lawrence This is a terrible situation.	**Friar** O woeful sympathy! Piteous predicament!
Nurse I know. Juliet is blubbering and weeping and weeping and blubbering. Stand up and be a man. For the sake of Juliet, stand up. Why should you be crying?	**Nurse** Even so lies she, Blubbering and weeping, weeping and blubbering.-- Stand up, stand up; stand, an you be a man: For Juliet's sake, for her sake, rise and stand; Why should you fall into so deep an O?
Romeo Nurse!	**Romeo** Nurse!
Nurse Death is the end for everyone.	**Nurse** Ah sir! ah sir!--Well, death's the end of all.
Romeo You spoke of Juliet. How is she? Does she see me as a murderer now? I have killed her relative and our joy. Where is she? What does she say about us?	**Romeo** Spakest thou of Juliet? how is it with her? Doth not she think me an old murderer, Now I have stain'd the childhood of our joy With blood remov'd but little from her own? Where is she? and how doth she/ and what says My conceal'd lady to our cancell'd love?
Nurse She doesn't say anything. She just cries and cries. She falls on her bed and cries for Tybalt and you. Then, she cries some more.	**Nurse** O, she says nothing, sir, but weeps and weeps; And now falls on her bed; and then starts up, And Tybalt calls; and then on Romeo cries, And then down falls again.
Romeo She cries for me and it is killing her, like I killed Tybalt. Tell me, Friar, what do I have to cut out to remove this sin? (Drawing his sword.)	**Romeo** As if that name, Shot from the deadly level of a gun, Did murder her; as that name's cursed hand Murder'd her kinsman.--O, tell me, friar, tell me, In what vile part of this anatomy Doth my name lodge? tell me, that I may sack The hateful mansion. [Drawing his sword.]
Friar Lawrence	**Friar**

Hold on. Aren't you a man? You are acting like a little girl or a wild beast. I thought you knew better. You have killed Tybalt, so are you going to kill yourself, too? That will kill Juliet for sure. Do not take your life for granted and curse your birth, the heavens, and the earth. You should be ashamed for even thinking of such a thing. You are nothing if you cannot take responsibility for your actions. You are like a ticking time bomb! Get up. Juliet is alive. She is the reason for part of this, because Tybalt was coming to kill you. So, you killed Tybalt. Be happy you are alive. The law has been ignored and instead of facing execution, you are facing banishment. You are blessed, but you refuse to see it. Listen to me. People like you die miserable. Go to Juliet. Comfort her, but do not stay too long. You must make your way to Mantua, where you will live until we can figure out a way for you to come back to rejoin your wife and friends. Beg the Prince's pardon and then you can come back and be happier than you ever were before. Go ahead, Nurse, and tell Juliet. Tell her to urge her family to bed after their long day of mourning. Tell her Romeo is coming.

Hold thy desperate hand: Art thou a man? thy form cries out thou art; Thy tears are womanish; thy wild acts denote The unreasonable fury of a beast; Unseemly woman in a seeming man! Or ill-beseeming beast in seeming both! Thou hast amaz'd me: by my holy order, I thought thy disposition better temper'd. Hast thou slain Tybalt? wilt thou slay thyself? And slay thy lady, too, that lives in thee, By doing damned hate upon thyself? Why rail'st thou on thy birth, the heaven, and earth? Since birth and heaven and earth, all three do meet In thee at once; which thou at once wouldst lose. Fie, fie, thou sham'st thy shape, thy love, thy wit; Which, like a usurer, abound'st in all, And usest none in that true use indeed Which should bedeck thy shape, thy love, thy wit: Thy noble shape is but a form of wax, Digressing from the valour of a man; Thy dear love sworn, but hollow perjury, Killing that love which thou hast vow'd to cherish; Thy wit, that ornament to shape and love, Mis-shapen in the conduct of them both, Like powder in a skilless soldier's flask, Is set a-fire by thine own ignorance, And thou dismember'd with thine own defence. What, rouse thee, man! thy Juliet is alive, For whose dear sake thou wast but lately dead; There art thou happy: Tybalt would kill thee, But thou slewest Tybalt; there art thou happy too: The law, that threaten'd death, becomes thy friend, And turns it to exile; there art thou happy: A pack of blessings lights upon thy back; Happiness courts thee in her best array; But, like a misbehav'd and sullen wench, Thou pout'st upon thy fortune and thy love:-- Take heed, take heed, for such die miserable. Go, get thee to thy love, as was decreed, Ascend her chamber, hence and comfort her: But, look, thou stay not till

Nurse
I could stay here all night and listen to your wise words. I will tell my lady you are coming.

Romeo
Please do, and tell her I am sorry.

Nurse
Here, sir, this is a ring she asked me to give you. Hurry! It's getting late.

(Exit Nurse.)

Romeo
I am feeling better.

Friar Lawrence
Go then and good night. Get out before the sun comes up and go to Mantua. Send your man to me from time to time and I will keep you posted about what is going on here. Give me your hand. It is late and you must go.

Romeo
Even though I am going to be filled with joy, I am sad to leave you. Farewell.

the watch be set, For then thou canst not pass to Mantua; Where thou shalt live till we can find a time To blaze your marriage, reconcile your friends, Beg pardon of the prince, and call thee back With twenty hundred thousand times more joy Than thou went'st forth in lamentation.-- Go before, nurse: commend me to thy lady; And bid her hasten all the house to bed, Which heavy sorrow makes them apt unto. Romeo is coming.

Nurse
O Lord, I could have stay'd here all the night To hear good counsel: O, what learning is!-- My lord, I'll tell my lady you will come.

Romeo
Do so, and bid my sweet prepare to chide.

Nurse
Here, sir, a ring she bid me give you, sir: Hie you, make haste, for it grows very late.

[Exit.]

Romeo
How well my comfort is reviv'd by this!

Friar
Go hence; good night! and here stands all your state: Either be gone before the watch be set, Or by the break of day disguis'd from hence. Sojourn in Mantua; I'll find out your man, And he shall signify from time to time Every good hap to you that chances here: Give me thy hand; 'tis late; farewell; good night.

Romeo
But that a joy past joy calls out on me, It were a grief so brief to part with thee:

(Exit all.)	Farewell. [Exeunt.]

Scene IV: A room in Capulet's house.

(Enter Capulet, Lady Capulet, and Paris.)

Capulet
Things have not gone well lately, so we have not had time to prepare Juliet for marriage. She loved Tybalt dearly, as I did, so she probably won't come down tonight. I would have gone to bed myself, if you weren't here.

Paris
I understand this is not the best time to try to win your daughter's affections. Please give her my best. Good night.

Lady Capulet
I will, and I will talk to her early tomorrow about you, but tonight she is too upset.

Capulet
Sir Paris, I will make her marry you. Wife, go to her now or go to bed. Tell her about Paris's love and inform her that she will be getting married Wednesday. What day is this, anyway?

Paris
Monday, sir.

Capulet
Monday! Ha-ha! Wednesday is too soon then. Make it Thursday, wife. She will be married to this noble earl. Paris, will you

Capulet
Things have fallen out, sir, so unluckily That we have had no time to move our daughter: Look you, she lov'd her kinsman Tybalt dearly, And so did I; well, we were born to die. 'Tis very late; she'll not come down to-night: I promise you, but for your company, I would have been a-bed an hour ago.

Paris
These times of woe afford no tune to woo.-- Madam, good night: commend me to your daughter.

Lady Capulet
I will, and know her mind early to-morrow; To-night she's mew'd up to her heaviness.

Capulet
Sir Paris, I will make a desperate tender Of my child's love: I think she will be rul'd In all respects by me; nay more, I doubt it not.-- Wife, go you to her ere you go to bed; Acquaint her here of my son Paris' love; And bid her, mark you me, on Wednesday next,-- But, soft! what day is this?

Paris
Monday, my lord.

Capulet
Monday! ha, ha! Well, Wednesday is too soon, Thursday let it be;--a Thursday, tell her, She shall be married to this noble

be ready? Is this too soon for you? We'll keep it intimate, just a few friends. If we celebrate too much, people will think we have no respect for the dead. So, we'll keep it simple. What do think about Thursday?

Paris
I wish Thursday were tomorrow.

Capulet
Well, go on. Thursday it is. Go, wife, to Juliet or go to bed. Let her know about her wedding arrangements. Farewell, my lord. It is almost morning now, so good night.

(Exit all.)

earl.-- Will you be ready? do you like this haste? We'll keep no great ado,--a friend or two; For, hark you, Tybalt being slain so late, It may be thought we held him carelessly, Being our kinsman, if we revel much: Therefore we'll have some half a dozen friends, And there an end. But what say you to Thursday?

Paris
My lord, I would that Thursday were to-morrow.

Capulet
Well, get you gone: o' Thursday be it then.-- Go you to Juliet, ere you go to bed, Prepare her, wife, against this wedding-day.-- Farewell, my lord.--Light to my chamber, ho!-- Afore me, it is so very very late That we may call it early by and by.-- Good night.

[Exeunt.]

Scene V: An open gallery to Juliet's chamber, overlooking the garden.

(Enter Romeo and Juliet.)

Juliet Will you be gone? It's not day yet. I heard the nightingale, the bird of night, not the lark, the bird of morning. Believe me it is not time to go.	**Juliet** Wilt thou be gone? it is not yet near day: It was the nightingale, and not the lark, That pierc'd the fearful hollow of thine ear; Nightly she sings on yond pomegranate tree: Believe me, love, it was the nightingale.
Romeo I heard the lark. I can see the sunrise just over the mountain tops. I must leave or stay and die.	**Romeo** It was the lark, the herald of the morn, No nightingale: look, love, what envious streaks Do lace the severing clouds in yonder east: Night's candles are burnt out, and jocund day Stands tiptoe on the misty mountain tops. I must be gone and live, or stay and die.
Juliet The light you see is not daylight, but some meteor from the sun to light up the night for you to make your way to Mantua. You still have time; don't leave.	**Juliet** Yond light is not daylight, I know it, I: It is some meteor that the sun exhales To be to thee this night a torch-bearer And light thee on the way to Mantua: Therefore stay yet, thou need'st not to be gone.
Romeo Let them take me then and put me to death, if that's what you want. I am content to stay with you. I will agree with you that the approaching light is not morning or the song we here comes from the lark. I would rather stay than go, no matter what happens. So, let's talk.	**Romeo** Let me be ta'en, let me be put to death; I am content, so thou wilt have it so. I'll say yon gray is not the morning's eye, 'Tis but the pale reflex of Cynthia's brow; Nor that is not the lark whose notes do beat The vaulty heaven so high above our heads: I have more care to stay than will to go.-- Come, death, and welcome! Juliet wills it so.-- How is't, my soul? let's talk,--it is not day.
Juliet No, you're right. It is day. Leave quickly! It is the lark singing the song that separates us. I	**Juliet** It is, it is!--hie hence, be gone, away! It is the lark that sings so out of tune, Straining harsh

hate the sound. Some say that the lark and toad traded eyes. I wish they had traded voices, too, since that voice represents our parting. Now, go. It is growing lighter and they will be hunting for you.

Romeo
The more light that comes, the darker we feel.

(Enter Nurse.)

Nurse
Madam!

Juliet
Nurse?

Nurse
Your mother is coming. Day is broken. Look out.

(Exit.)

Juliet
You must go out the window.

Romeo
Farewell, farewell. One more kiss, and I'll go.

(Descends.)

Juliet
Are you gone my love, my life, my friend? I must hear from you every minute of every day. It will be years before we are together again.

Romeo
Goodbye. I will send word and my love every

discords and unpleasing sharps. Some say the lark makes sweet division; This doth not so, for she divideth us: Some say the lark and loathed toad change eyes; O, now I would they had chang'd voices too! Since arm from arm that voice doth us affray, Hunting thee hence with hunt's-up to the day. O, now be gone; more light and light it grows.

Romeo
More light and light,--more dark and dark our woes!

[Enter Nurse.]

Nurse
Madam!

Juliet
Nurse?

Nurse
Your lady mother is coming to your chamber: The day is broke; be wary, look about.

[Exit.]

Juliet
Then, window, let day in, and let life out.

Romeo
Farewell, farewell! one kiss, and I'll descend.

[Descends.]

Juliet
Art thou gone so? my lord, my love, my friend! I must hear from thee every day i' the hour, For in a minute there are many days: O, by this count I shall be much in years Ere I again behold my Romeo!

Romeo
Farewell! I will omit no opportunity That may

chance I get.

Juliet
Do you think we will ever meet again?

Romeo
I have no doubt. All these terrible things will be mere memories for us to share in our old age.

Juliet
Oh God! I feel like I am looking at you at the bottom of your tomb. Either my eyes are playing tricks on me, or you look really pale.

Romeo
Trust me, love, you look pale, too. Our sadness makes us sick. Goodbye, goodbye!

(Exit Romeo.)

Juliet
Oh strange fate! What are you doing to him? If you are fickle, please send him back soon.

Lady Capulet
(From inside.) Hello, daughter! Are you up?

Juliet
Who is it? Is it my mother? She never stays up so late or gets up so early. What does she want?

(Enter Lady Capulet.)

Lady Capulet
What's wrong, Juliet?

Juliet
I don't feel well.

---

convey my greetings, love, to thee.

Juliet
O, think'st thou we shall ever meet again?

Romeo
I doubt it not; and all these woes shall serve For sweet discourses in our time to come.

Juliet
O God! I have an ill-divining soul! Methinks I see thee, now thou art below, As one dead in the bottom of a tomb: Either my eyesight fails, or thou look'st pale.

Romeo
And trust me, love, in my eye so do you: Dry sorrow drinks our blood. Adieu, adieu!

[Exit below.]

Juliet
O fortune, fortune! all men call thee fickle: If thou art fickle, what dost thou with him That is renown'd for faith? Be fickle, fortune; For then, I hope, thou wilt not keep him long But send him back.

Lady Capulet
[Within.] Ho, daughter! are you up?

Juliet
Who is't that calls? is it my lady mother? Is she not down so late, or up so early? What unaccustom'd cause procures her hither?

[Enter Lady Capulet.]

Lady Capulet
Why, how now, Juliet?

Juliet
Madam, I am not well.

Lady Capulet Are you still crying over your cousin's death? You can't bring him back with tears. And, if you could, you couldn't keep him alive. So, stop crying. A little grief is okay, but too much is ridiculous.	**Lady Capulet** Evermore weeping for your cousin's death? What, wilt thou wash him from his grave with tears? An if thou couldst, thou couldst not make him live; Therefore have done: some grief shows much of love; But much of grief shows still some want of wit.
Juliet I am crying because I feel a great loss.	**Juliet** Yet let me weep for such a feeling loss.
Lady Capulet You feel a loss, but Tybalt feels nothing.	**Lady Capulet** So shall you feel the loss, but not the friend Which you weep for.
Juliet I feel like I will cry forever.	**Juliet** Feeling so the loss, I cannot choose but ever weep the friend.
Lady Capulet You are crying because of Tybalt's death and because his murderer is still alive.	**Lady Capulet** Well, girl, thou weep'st not so much for his death As that the villain lives which slaughter'd him.
Juliet What murderer, madam?	**Juliet** What villain, madam?
Lady Capulet Romeo.	**Lady Capulet** That same villain Romeo.
Juliet (To herself.) He is not a murderer or a villain. God forgive him. I know I do, with all of my heart. My heart aches for him.	**Juliet** Villain and he be many miles asunder.-- God pardon him! I do, with all my heart; And yet no man like he doth grieve my heart.
Lady Capulet Because the murderer is alive.	**Lady Capulet** That is because the traitor murderer lives.
Juliet Yes, ma'am. I would kill him myself, if I could put my hands on him.	**Juliet** Ay, madam, from the reach of these my hands. Would none but I might venge my cousin's death!

Lady Capulet Don't worry. We will have our revenge. Don't cry anymore. I am going to send someone to Mantua, where Romeo is and have him dealt with. Then, you'll feel better.	**Lady Capulet** We will have vengeance for it, fear thou not: Then weep no more. I'll send to one in Mantua,-- Where that same banish'd runagate doth live,-- Shall give him such an unaccustom'd dram That he shall soon keep Tybalt company: And then I hope thou wilt be satisfied.
Juliet I will never be okay, until I see Romeo dead. If you could find someone to take him a poison, I would mix it myself. My heart hates to hear his name and not be able to go after him. I want to take out my frustrations on his body.	**Juliet** Indeed I never shall be satisfied With Romeo till I behold him--dead-- Is my poor heart so for a kinsman vex'd: Madam, if you could find out but a man To bear a poison, I would temper it, That Romeo should, upon receipt thereof, Soon sleep in quiet. O, how my heart abhors To hear him nam'd,--and cannot come to him,-- To wreak the love I bore my cousin Tybalt Upon his body that hath slaughter'd him!
Lady Capulet If you could find a way, I'll find the man. But now, I have some great news.	**Lady Capulet** Find thou the means, and I'll find such a man. But now I'll tell thee joyful tidings, girl.
Juliet I need some good news. What is it? Tell me.	**Juliet** And joy comes well in such a needy time: What are they, I beseech your ladyship?
Lady Capulet Well, you know you have a very wise father. He wants to help you get over Tybalt's death with a joyous occasion you haven't even thought about.	**Lady Capulet** Well, well, thou hast a careful father, child; One who, to put thee from thy heaviness, Hath sorted out a sudden day of joy That thou expect'st not, nor I look'd not for.
Juliet Madam, tell me quickly, on what day is it?	**Juliet** Madam, in happy time, what day is that?
Lady Capulet Thursday morning, you will marry the noble Paris at St. Peter's Church.	**Lady Capulet** Marry, my child, early next Thursday morn The gallant, young, and noble gentleman, The County Paris, at St. Peter's Church, Shall happily make thee there a joyful bride.
Juliet I will not marry him. What is the hurry? He	**Juliet** Now by Saint Peter's Church, and Peter too, He

hasn't even asked me out. Please, tell my father I would rather marry Romeo, whom you know I hate, than marry Paris.

Lady Capulet
Well, here comes your father. You can tell him yourself and see how he takes it.

(Enter Capulet and Nurse.)

Capulet
When the sun sets, dew comes, but on the night of my brother's son's death, it rains. What is wrong now, girl? Are you still crying? You must be a fountain with all the tears you've shed. You must calm down. Have you told her the news?

Lady Capulet
Yes sir, I told her. But she won't hear of it. She says no thanks! I wish she were dead.

Capulet
Don't say that. I don't understand. How can she be so ungrateful? Does she not have any pride? Doesn't she know how blessed she is to be able to marry such a gentleman?

Juliet
I am not proud of whom you have found, but I am thankful that you cared so much to look. I know you meant it lovingly, but I do not have to

shall not make me there a joyful bride. I wonder at this haste; that I must wed Ere he that should be husband comes to woo. I pray you, tell my lord and father, madam, I will not marry yet; and when I do, I swear It shall be Romeo, whom you know I hate, Rather than Paris:-- these are news indeed!

Lady Capulet
Here comes your father: tell him so yourself, And see how he will take it at your hands.

[Enter Capulet and Nurse.]

Capulet
When the sun sets, the air doth drizzle dew; But for the sunset of my brother's son It rains downright.-- How now! a conduit, girl? what, still in tears? Evermore showering? In one little body Thou counterfeit'st a bark, a sea, a wind: For still thy eyes, which I may call the sea, Do ebb and flow with tears; the bark thy body is, Sailing in this salt flood; the winds, thy sighs; Who,--raging with thy tears and they with them,-- Without a sudden calm, will overset Thy tempest-tossed body.--How now, wife! Have you deliver'd to her our decree?

Lady Capulet
Ay, sir; but she will none, she gives you thanks. I would the fool were married to her grave!

Capulet
Soft! take me with you, take me with you, wife. How! will she none? doth she not give us thanks? Is she not proud? doth she not count her bles'd, Unworthy as she is, that we have wrought So worthy a gentleman to be her bridegroom?

Juliet
Not proud you have; but thankful that you have: Proud can I never be of what I hate; But thankful even for hate that is meant love.

love what you did.

Capulet
What? What logic are you using? Proud, and I thank you, and I thank you not. Regardless of how you feel, you are going to be married Thursday at Saint Peter's Church, even if I have to drag you there. Now, get out of here, you sick girl.

Lady Capulet
Have you lost your mind?

Juliet
Please, father! I am begging you! Hear me out.

Capulet
No, you disobedient wretch! Get yourself to the church on Thursday or never look at me again. Don't say another word to me. I can barely keep myself from slapping you. Wife, we never thought we were too blessed, only having one child. Now, I see we were cursed, and one was too much.

Nurse
Bless her, Lord! Do not treat her like this.

Capulet
Why not, wise woman? Hold your tongue or go spread more gossip with your friends.

Nurse
I've not said anything wrong.

Capulet
Oh, God have mercy.

Capulet
How now, how now, chop-logic! What is this? Proud,--and, I thank you,--and I thank you not;-- And yet not proud:--mistress minion, you, Thank me no thankings, nor proud me no prouds, But fettle your fine joints 'gainst Thursday next To go with Paris to Saint Peter's Church, Or I will drag thee on a hurdle thither. Out, you green-sickness carrion! out, you baggage! You tallow-face!

Lady Capulet
Fie, fie! what, are you mad?

Juliet
Good father, I beseech you on my knees, Hear me with patience but to speak a word.

Capulet
Hang thee, young baggage! disobedient wretch! I tell thee what,--get thee to church o' Thursday, Or never after look me in the face: Speak not, reply not, do not answer me; My fingers itch.-- Wife, we scarce thought us bles'd That God had lent us but this only child; But now I see this one is one too much, And that we have a curse in having her: Out on her, hilding!

Nurse
God in heaven bless her!-- You are to blame, my lord, to rate her so.

Capulet
And why, my lady wisdom? hold your tongue, Good prudence; smatter with your gossips, go.

Nurse
I speak no treason.

Capulet
O, God ye good-en!

Nurse May I speak?	**Nurse** May not one speak?
Capulet Be quiet fool! We do not need to hear any of your gibberish.	**Capulet** Peace, you mumbling fool! Utter your gravity o'er a gossip's bowl, For here we need it not.
Lady Capulet You are getting over-steamed.	**Lady Capulet** You are too hot.
Capulet I swear it makes me mad! No matter what I was doing, all I ever wanted was to find her a suitable husband. And when I find one she says, "I'm too young to get married. Please excuse me." Well, I'll excuse you from this house, if you won't get married. You may find another place to eat and sleep. You better look at this thing clearly, because I'm not joking. Thursday is near, so be advised, I am giving you away to my friend. You will not deny me or I will let you die, starve, or beg in the streets. Don't test me on this. (Exit.)	**Capulet** God's bread! it makes me mad: Day, night, hour, time, tide, work, play, Alone, in company, still my care hath been To have her match'd, and having now provided A gentleman of noble parentage, Of fair demesnes, youthful, and nobly train'd, Stuff'd, as they say, with honourable parts, Proportion'd as one's heart would wish a man,-- And then to have a wretched puling fool, A whining mammet, in her fortune's tender, To answer, 'I'll not wed,--I cannot love, I am too young,--I pray you pardon me:'-- But, an you will not wed, I'll pardon you: Graze where you will, you shall not house with me: Look to't, think on't, I do not use to jest. Thursday is near; lay hand on heart, advise: An you be mine, I'll give you to my friend; An you be not, hang, beg, starve, die i' the streets, For, by my soul, I'll ne'er acknowledge thee, Nor what is mine shall never do thee good: Trust to't, bethink you, I'll not be forsworn. [Exit.]
Juliet Doesn't anyone have pity for me? Oh sweet mother, do not throw me away? Delay this marriage for a month or a week. Otherwise, make my marriage bed in the vault with Tybalt.	**Juliet** Is there no pity sitting in the clouds, That sees into the bottom of my grief? O, sweet my mother, cast me not away! Delay this marriage for a month, a week; Or, if you do not, make the bridal bed In that dim monument where Tybalt lies.
Lady Capulet Do not talk to me, because I have nothing to	**Lady Capulet** Talk not to me, for I'll not speak a word; Do as

say. Do as you will; I am done with you.

(Exit.)

Juliet
Oh God! Oh Nurse! How can this mess be prevented? I already have a husband on earth and I believe in the word of God. How can I get married again while he is living? Help me! Tell me what to do! Why does something like this have to happen to someone like me? What do you have to say, Nurse? Give me some comfort.

Nurse
Romeo is banished and he cannot come back and challenge this marriage. If he does, he can't be seen. So, you better follow through with this marriage. Paris is a wonderful gentleman and Romeo doesn't compare. Madam, an eagle's eyes are not as green as Paris's. I swear you will be happy with this second match. It will be so much better than your first. Your first husband is dead or as good as dead.

Juliet
Are you speaking from your heart?

Nurse
And my soul, too. I swear.

Juliet
Amen!

Nurse
What?

Juliet
Well, you have made me feel better. Please, tell my mother since I have angered my father, I

thou wilt, for I have done with thee.

[Exit.]

Juliet
O God!--O nurse! how shall this be prevented? My husband is on earth, my faith in heaven; How shall that faith return again to earth, Unless that husband send it me from heaven By leaving earth?--comfort me, counsel me.-- Alack, alack, that heaven should practise stratagems Upon so soft a subject as myself!-- What say'st thou? hast thou not a word of joy? Some comfort, nurse.

Nurse
Faith, here 'tis; Romeo Is banished; and all the world to nothing That he dares ne'er come back to challenge you; Or if he do, it needs must be by stealth. Then, since the case so stands as now it doth, I think it best you married with the county. O, he's a lovely gentleman! Romeo's a dishclout to him; an eagle, madam, Hath not so green, so quick, so fair an eye As Paris hath. Beshrew my very heart, I think you are happy in this second match, For it excels your first: or if it did not, Your first is dead; or 'twere as good he were, As living here, and you no use of him.

Juliet
Speakest thou this from thy heart?

Nurse
And from my soul too; Or else beshrew them both.

Juliet
Amen!

Nurse
What?

Juliet
Well, thou hast comforted me marvellous much.

have gone to Friar Lawrence's cell to make confession and be absolved.

Nurse
I will. That is a good idea.

(Exit Nurse.)

Juliet
Damn her! Wicked woman! How dare she speak that way about my husband and with the same mouth she used to praise him? Go, counselor! I will never tell you anything again. I'll go to the friar and see what he thinks I should do. If nothing else, I will kill myself.

(Exit.)

Go in; and tell my lady I am gone, Having displeas'd my father, to Lawrence' cell, To make confession and to be absolv'd.

Nurse
Marry, I will; and this is wisely done.

[Exit.]

Juliet
Ancient damnation! O most wicked fiend! Is it more sin to wish me thus forsworn, Or to dispraise my lord with that same tongue Which she hath prais'd him with above compare So many thousand times?--Go, counsellor; Thou and my bosom henceforth shall be twain.-- I'll to the friar to know his remedy; If all else fail, myself have power to die.

[Exit.]

Act IV

Scene I: Friar Lawrence's Cell

(Enter Friar Lawrence and Paris.)

Friar Lawrence On Thursday, sir? That doesn't give you much time.	**Friar** On Thursday, sir? the time is very short.
Paris My soon-to-be father-in-law, Capulet, wants it done quickly. So, I see no reason to stop him.	**Paris** My father Capulet will have it so; And I am nothing slow to slack his haste.
Friar Lawrence But, you say you barely know the lady. That makes me think it is not such a good idea to rush into things.	**Friar** You say you do not know the lady's mind: Uneven is the course; I like it not.
Paris She is grieving the death of her cousin Tybalt, so I haven't had time to really win her affections. The goddess of love, Venus, cannot work her magic on someone in mourning. I think that is the reason her father is in such a hurry, to help her heal. She will not cry so much with me around.	**Paris** Immoderately she weeps for Tybalt's death, And therefore have I little talk'd of love; For Venus smiles not in a house of tears. Now, sir, her father counts it dangerous That she do give her sorrow so much sway; And, in his wisdom, hastes our marriage, To stop the inundation of her tears; Which, too much minded by herself alone, May be put from her by society: Now do you know the reason of this haste.
Friar Lawrence (To himself.) I wish I didn't know why this marriage can't happen. (To Paris.) Look, sir, here comes the lady toward my home. (Enter Juliet.)	**Friar** [Aside.] I would I knew not why it should be slow'd.-- Look, sir, here comes the lady toward my cell. [Enter Juliet.]
Paris It's so good to see you, my lady, my wife!	**Paris** Happily met, my lady and my wife!

Juliet
It will be good to see you, sir, when I am able to become a wife.

Paris
You must be ready by Thursday.

Juliet
What must be must be.

Friar Lawrence
So true.

Paris
Are you here to make confession?

Juliet
I should confess to you.

Paris
Do not deny your love for me.

Juliet
I will not deny that I am in love.

Paris
I'm sure you will tell him you are in love with me.

Juliet
If I do, it will be more meaningful if I do it in private.

Paris
You poor thing, your face shows how much you've been crying.

Juliet
Tears have little to do with how my face looks. It always looks like this.

Juliet
That may be, sir, when I may be a wife.

Paris
That may be must be, love, on Thursday next.

Juliet
What must be shall be.

Friar
That's a certain text.

Paris
Come you to make confession to this father?

Juliet
To answer that, I should confess to you.

Paris
Do not deny to him that you love me.

Juliet
I will confess to you that I love him.

Paris
So will ye, I am sure, that you love me.

Juliet
If I do so, it will be of more price, Being spoke behind your back than to your face.

Paris
Poor soul, thy face is much abus'd with tears.

Juliet
The tears have got small victory by that; For it was bad enough before their spite.

Paris
That is not true.

Juliet
I am telling the truth about my face to your face.

Paris
Your face is mine and I will not have you talking ugly about it.

Juliet
My face is definitely not my own. May I speak with you, holy father? Or, should I come back at evening mass?

Friar Lawrence
No, now is fine. Paris, my lord, we must have some privacy.

Paris
God forbid I should disturb devotion. Until Thursday, Juliet. Goodbye, and until then remember this holy kiss.

(Exit Paris.)

Juliet
Oh, shut the door and come cry with me. I am hopelessly without cure or help!

Friar Lawrence
Ah, Juliet, I already know your grief. I have racked my brain trying to figure out a way for you to get out of this marriage, but you must marry this man on Thursday.

Juliet
Please don't tell me you know about it; tell me what we're going to do. Or, I will

Paris
Thou wrong'st it more than tears with that report.

Juliet
That is no slander, sir, which is a truth;
And what I spake, I spake it to my face.

Paris
Thy face is mine, and thou hast slander'd it.

Juliet
It may be so, for it is not mine own.-- Are you at leisure, holy father, now; Or shall I come to you at evening mass?

Friar
My leisure serves me, pensive daughter, now.-- My lord, we must entreat the time alone.

Paris
God shield I should disturb devotion!-- Juliet, on Thursday early will I rouse you: Till then, adieu; and keep this holy kiss.

[Exit.]

Juliet
O, shut the door! and when thou hast done so, Come weep with me; past hope, past cure, past help!

Friar
Ah, Juliet, I already know thy grief; It strains me past the compass of my wits: I hear thou must, and nothing may prorogue it, On Thursday next be married to this county.

Juliet
Tell me not, friar, that thou hear'st of this, Unless thou tell me how I may prevent it:

use this knife to prevent this marriage. Please give me some advice or watch me die.

If, in thy wisdom, thou canst give no help, Do thou but call my resolution wise, And with this knife I'll help it presently. God join'd my heart and Romeo's, thou our hands; And ere this hand, by thee to Romeo's seal'd, Shall be the label to another deed, Or my true heart with treacherous revolt Turn to another, this shall slay them both: Therefore, out of thy long-experienc'd time, Give me some present counsel; or, behold, 'Twixt my extremes and me this bloody knife Shall play the empire; arbitrating that Which the commission of thy years and art Could to no issue of true honour bring. Be not so long to speak; I long to die, If what thou speak'st speak not of remedy.

Friar Lawrence
Hold on. I may have an idea, but it will take some desperate measures to prevent this marriage. If you are willing to really kill yourself before you get married again, then you will probably go along with my idea.

Friar
Hold, daughter. I do spy a kind of hope, Which craves as desperate an execution As that is desperate which we would prevent. If, rather than to marry County Paris Thou hast the strength of will to slay thyself, Then is it likely thou wilt undertake A thing like death to chide away this shame, That cop'st with death himself to scape from it; And, if thou dar'st, I'll give thee remedy.

Juliet
I would rather leap to my death, or become a thief, or live with serpents, than marry Paris. I will do whatever it takes to prevent this marriage and stay true to my love.

Juliet
O, bid me leap, rather than marry Paris, From off the battlements of yonder tower; Or walk in thievish ways; or bid me lurk Where serpents are; chain me with roaring bears; Or shut me nightly in a charnel-house, O'er-cover'd quite with dead men's rattling bones, With reeky shanks and yellow chapless skulls; Or bid me go into a new-made grave, And hide me with a dead man in his shroud; Things that, to hear them told, have made me tremble; And I will do it without fear or doubt, To live an unstain'd wife to my sweet love.

Friar Lawrence

Go home then, act happy, and tell your parents you agree to marry Paris. Tomorrow night, make sure you are alone. Take this vial and drink it. You will fall into a deep sleep, and appear to have no breath or pulse. You will appear cold and lifeless, and even the color from your face will fade. You will remain like this for forty-two hours, so when your new husband comes to find you, he will think you are dead. You will be put into the Capulet's death vault. In the meantime, I will send Romeo word of our plan. He and I will be with you when you wake, and the two of you may go to Mantua. Can you go through with this plan?

Juliet

Of course, I can. Give me! Give me!

Friar Lawrence

(Giving her the vial.) Here, now go and stay strong. I'll send word to Romeo.

Friar

Hold, then; go home, be merry, give consent To marry Paris: Wednesday is to-morrow; To-morrow night look that thou lie alone, Let not thy nurse lie with thee in thy chamber: Take thou this vial, being then in bed, And this distilled liquor drink thou off: When, presently, through all thy veins shall run A cold and drowsy humour; for no pulse Shall keep his native progress, but surcease: No warmth, no breath, shall testify thou livest; The roses in thy lips and cheeks shall fade To paly ashes; thy eyes' windows fall, Like death, when he shuts up the day of life; Each part, depriv'd of supple government, Shall, stiff and stark and cold, appear like death: And in this borrow'd likeness of shrunk death Thou shalt continue two-and-forty hours, And then awake as from a pleasant sleep. Now, when the bridegroom in the morning comes To rouse thee from thy bed, there art thou dead: Then,--as the manner of our country is,-- In thy best robes, uncover'd, on the bier, Thou shalt be borne to that same ancient vault Where all the kindred of the Capulets lie. In the mean time, against thou shalt awake, Shall Romeo by my letters know our drift; And hither shall he come: and he and I Will watch thy waking, and that very night Shall Romeo bear thee hence to Mantua. And this shall free thee from this present shame, If no inconstant toy nor womanish fear Abate thy valour in the acting it.

Juliet

Give me, give me! O, tell not me of fear!

Friar

Hold; get you gone, be strong and prosperous In this resolve: I'll send a friar with speed To Mantua, with my letters to

Juliet Love give me strength, and strength help me get through this. Goodbye, dear Father. (Exit all.)	thy lord. **Juliet** Love give me strength! and strength shall help afford. Farewell, dear father. [Exeunt.]

Scene II: Hall in Capulet's house.

(Enter Capulet, Lady Capulet, Nurse, and Servants.)

Capulet Here, invite the guests on this list. (Exit first Servant.) Sir, go find and hire twenty chefs.	**Capulet** So many guests invite as here are writ.-- [Exit first Servant.] Sirrah, go hire me twenty cunning cooks.
Second Servant I will get only the best. I'll test them by making them lick their fingers.	**2 Servant** You shall have none ill, sir; for I'll try if they can lick their fingers.
Capulet How does that test them?	**Capulet** How canst thou try them so?
Second Servant Only good cooks can lick their fingers. Anyone who cannot will not come with me.	**2 Servant** Marry, sir, 'tis an ill cook that cannot lick his own fingers: therefore he that cannot lick his fingers goes not with me.
Capulet Well, go already. (Exit second Servant.) We are not going to be prepared for this wedding in time. Where is my daughter, Friar Lawrence's?	**Capulet** Go, begone.-- [Exit second Servant.] We shall be much unfurnish'd for this time.--What, is my daughter gone to Friar Lawrence?
Nurse Yes, true.	**Nurse** Ay, forsooth.
Capulet Good, I hope he has some influence on that spoiled brat.	**Capulet** Well, be may chance to do some good on her: A peevish self-will'd harlotry it is.
Nurse	**Nurse**

Here she comes now with a smile on her face.

(Enter Juliet.)

Capulet
Where have you been, my headstrong daughter?

Juliet
I have been where I could repent the sin of disobedience to my parents. Now, at Friar Lawrence's urgings, I am here to beg your forgiveness. (On her knees.) Please, forgive me. From now on, I will listen to you and do whatever you wish.

Capulet
Send for the Count. Tell him he is to wed tomorrow morning.

Juliet
I saw him at Friar Lawrence's cell and told him how I felt without being too forthcoming.

Capulet
That is good. Stand up. Everything is as it should be. Now, go fetch Paris and bring him here. We all owe the friar for this one.

Juliet
Nurse, will you go with me to my closet and help pick out the wedding attire for tomorrow?

Lady Capulet
There's plenty of time. The wedding is not until Thursday.

Capulet
Go Nurse, go with her. We are going to have

See where she comes from shrift with merry look.

[Enter Juliet.]

Capulet
How now, my headstrong! where have you been gadding?

Juliet
Where I have learn'd me to repent the sin Of disobedient opposition To you and your behests; and am enjoin'd By holy Lawrence to fall prostrate here, To beg your pardon:-- pardon, I beseech you! Henceforward I am ever rul'd by you.

Capulet
Send for the county; go tell him of this: I'll have this knot knit up to-morrow morning.

Juliet
I met the youthful lord at Lawrence' cell; And gave him what becomed love I might, Not stepping o'er the bounds of modesty.

Capulet
Why, I am glad on't; this is well,--stand up,-- This is as't should be.--Let me see the county; Ay, marry, go, I say, and fetch him hither.-- Now, afore God, this reverend holy friar, All our whole city is much bound to him.

Juliet
Nurse, will you go with me into my closet, To help me sort such needful ornaments As you think fit to furnish me to-morrow?

Lady Capulet
No, not till Thursday; there is time enough.

Capulet
Go, nurse, go with her.--We'll to church to-

the wedding tomorrow.

(Exit Juliet and Nurse.)

Lady Capulet
We are not going to have enough food for the party. It's almost night.

Capulet
Don't worry. I will get things ready. I promise. Go help Juliet get ready. I'll be working all night so don't expect me to come to bed. I'll be the housewife for once. Where is everyone? I will go get Paris myself and prepare him for tomorrow. I feel like a heavy weight has been lifted now that my wayward daughter is going to be married.

(Exit Capulet.)

morrow.

[Exeunt Juliet and Nurse.]

Lady Capulet
We shall be short in our provision: 'Tis now near night.

Capulet
Tush, I will stir about, And all things shall be well, I warrant thee, wife: Go thou to Juliet, help to deck up her; I'll not to bed to-night;--let me alone; I'll play the housewife for this once.-- What, ho!-- They are all forth: well, I will walk myself To County Paris, to prepare him up Against to-morrow: my heart is wondrous light Since this same wayward girl is so reclaim'd.

[Exeunt.]

Scene III: Juliet's bedroom.

(Enter Juliet and Nurse.)

Juliet
Those outfits are best, but gentle Nurse, I need to be alone now. I need time to pray for blessings upon tomorrow because you know I am full of sin.

(Enter Lady Capulet.)

Lady Capulet
Are you busy? Do you need my help?

Juliet
No ma'am. We have figured everything out. So, if you don't mind, I want to be alone. Let the Nurse stay with you tonight, because I know how busy you are with the preparations.

Lady Capulet
Good night then. Go to bed and get some rest because you are going to need it.

(Exit Lady Capulet and Nurse.)

Juliet
Goodnight. God only knows when we will see each other again. I am cold with fear. Maybe I'll call them back. Nurse! Oh, what good can she do me? I must do this alone. Here is the vial. What if this doesn't work? What if I have to get married tomorrow? I will lay my knife beside me in case it doesn't. What if this is a poison the friar has given me so he will not be dishonored, because he married me to Romeo? No, he would not do such a terrible thing

Juliet
Ay, those attires are best:--but, gentle nurse, I pray thee, leave me to myself to-night; For I have need of many orisons To move the heavens to smile upon my state, Which, well thou know'st, is cross and full of sin.

[Enter Lady Capulet.]

Lady Capulet
What, are you busy, ho? need you my help?

Juliet
No, madam; we have cull'd such necessaries As are behoveful for our state to-morrow: So please you, let me now be left alone, And let the nurse this night sit up with you; For I am sure you have your hands full all In this so sudden business.

Lady Capulet
Good night: Get thee to bed, and rest; for thou hast need.

[Exeunt Lady Capulet and Nurse.]

Juliet
Farewell!--God knows when we shall meet again. I have a faint cold fear thrills through my veins That almost freezes up the heat of life: I'll call them back again to comfort me;-- Nurse!-- What should she do here? My dismal scene I needs must act alone.-- Come, vial.-- What if this mixture do not work at all? Shall I be married, then, to-morrow morning?-- No, No!-- this shall forbid it:--lie thou there.--

because he is a righteous man. I will not think negatively of him. What if I wake up in the tomb before Romeo gets there? Will I suffocate in the vault? Or, if I live, be surrounded by the terror of death and darkness, and the dead, decomposing bodies of my ancestors. Perhaps, Tybalt, just now laid to rest, will stir like they say of new spirits. So if I wake early, the terrible smells and spirits' howls will drive me crazy. I will play with the joints of my ancestors, try to wake Tybalt, and finally bash my brains out with a bone. I think I see Tybalt now, looking for Romeo, his murderer. Stay Tybalt, stay. Romeo, I am coming. I drink to you.

(Throws herself on the bed.)

[Laying down her dagger.]

What if it be a poison, which the friar Subtly hath minister'd to have me dead, Lest in this marriage he should be dishonour'd, Because he married me before to Romeo? I fear it is: and yet methinks it should not, For he hath still been tried a holy man:-- I will not entertain so bad a thought.-- How if, when I am laid into the tomb, I wake before the time that Romeo Come to redeem me? there's a fearful point! Shall I not then be stifled in the vault, To whose foul mouth no healthsome air breathes in, And there die strangled ere my Romeo comes? Or, if I live, is it not very like The horrible conceit of death and night, Together with the terror of the place,-- As in a vault, an ancient receptacle, Where, for this many hundred years, the bones Of all my buried ancestors are pack'd; Where bloody Tybalt, yet but green in earth, Lies festering in his shroud; where, as they say, At some hours in the night spirits resort;-- Alack, alack, is it not like that I, So early waking,-- what with loathsome smells, And shrieks like mandrakes torn out of the earth, That living mortals, hearing them, run mad;-- O, if I wake, shall I not be distraught, Environed with all these hideous fears? And madly play with my forefathers' joints? And pluck the mangled Tybalt from his shroud? And, in this rage, with some great kinsman's bone, As with a club, dash out my desperate brains?-- O, look! methinks I see my cousin's ghost Seeking out Romeo, that did spit his body Upon a rapier's point:--stay, Tybalt, stay!-- Romeo, I come! this do I drink to thee.

[Throws herself on the bed.]

Scene IV: Hall in Capulet's house.

(Enter Lady Capulet and Nurse.)

Lady Capulet Nurse, hold these keys and go get more spices.	**Lady Capulet** Hold, take these keys and fetch more spices, nurse.
Nurse The recipe calls for dates and quinces.	**Nurse** They call for dates and quinces in the pastry.
(Enter Capulet.)	[Enter Capulet.]
Capulet Hurry, hurry! It's three o'clock already. Get the meats ready, Angelica. Don't worry about the costs.	**Capulet** Come, stir, stir, stir! The second cock hath crow'd, The curfew bell hath rung, 'tis three o'clock:-- Look to the bak'd meats, good Angelica; Spare not for cost.
Nurse Go to bed, you old housewife. You'll be sick tomorrow, if you stay up all night.	**Nurse** Go, you cot-quean, go, Get you to bed; faith, you'll be sick to-morrow For this night's watching.
Capulet Nonsense! I have stayed up all night before for much lesser reasons and not been sick.	**Capulet** No, not a whit: what! I have watch'd ere now All night for lesser cause, and ne'er been sick.
Lady Capulet Yes, you used to chase the ladies once upon a time, but I'll make sure you don't anymore.	**Lady Capulet** Ay, you have been a mouse-hunt in your time; But I will watch you from such watching now.
(Exit Lady Capulet and Nurse.)	[Exeunt Lady Capulet and Nurse.]
Capulet Jealous, jealous woman. Now, fellow…	**Capulet** A jealous-hood, a jealous-hood!--Now, fellow,
(Enter Servants, with spits, logs and baskets.)	[Enter Servants, with spits, logs and baskets.]
…what do you have there?	What's there?

First Servant Stuff for the cook, sir. I'm not sure what it is.	**1 Servant** Things for the cook, sir; but I know not what.
Capulet Well, hurry up. (Exit first Servant.) Sir, go get drier logs. Peter can tell you where they are.	**Capulet** Make haste, make haste. [Exit 1 Servant.] -- Sirrah, fetch drier logs: Call Peter, he will show thee where they are.
Second Servant I'm not dense, sir. I can find the logs without Peter's help. (Exit second Servant.)	**2 Servant** I have a head, sir, that will find out logs And never trouble Peter for the matter. [Exit.]
Capulet Right, good fellow. He's funny. Oh my, it is already daylight. Paris will be here with the music soon. I think I hear him coming. (Music plays within.) Nurse! Wife! Nurse! (Enter Nurse.) Go wake Juliet. Get her ready. I'll go and chat with Paris. Hurry up! The groom is here already. Hurry up, I say. (Exit all.)	**Capulet** Mass, and well said; a merry whoreson, ha! Thou shalt be logger-head.--Good faith, 'tis day. The county will be here with music straight, For so he said he would:--I hear him near. [Music within.] Nurse!--wife!--what, ho!--what, nurse, I say! [Re-enter Nurse.] Go, waken Juliet; go and trim her up; I'll go and chat with Paris:--hie, make haste, Make haste; the bridegroom he is come already: Make haste, I say. [Exeunt.]

Scene V: Juliet's bedroom with Juliet lying on the bed.

(Enter Nurse.)

Nurse

Miss! Miss! Juliet! Hurry, you sleepyhead! Your love has arrived. Wake up, bride! What not a word? Do you want to sleep because you know with Paris, you will not get much sleep? God forgive me! She is sound asleep and I hate to wake her, but I must. Madam, madam! The Count will wake you up soon enough. Are you dressed already and asleep again? You must wake up, lady! Oh, no! My lady is dead! Help! Oh, curse the day I was born! Someone get me a drink! My lord! My lady!

(Enter Lady Capulet.)

Lady Capulet

What is all the noise in here?

Nurse

It is a sad day!

Lady Capulet

What is the matter?

Nurse

Look, look! Oh what a terrible day!

Lady Capulet

Oh me, oh me! My child, my only child! Wake her up or I will die right here! Help, help! Get some help!

Nurse

Mistress!--what, mistress!--Juliet!--fast, I warrant her, she:-- Why, lamb!--why, lady!--fie, you slug-abed!-- Why, love, I say!--madam! sweetheart!--why, bride!-- What, not a word?-- you take your pennyworths now; Sleep for a week; for the next night, I warrant, The County Paris hath set up his rest That you shall rest but little.--God forgive me! Marry, and amen, how sound is she asleep! I needs must wake her.-- Madam, madam, madam!-- Ay, let the county take you in your bed; He'll fright you up, i' faith.--Will it not be? What, dress'd! and in your clothes! and down again! I must needs wake you.--lady! lady! lady!-- Alas, alas!--Help, help! My lady's dead!-- O, well-a-day that ever I was born!-- Some aqua-vitae, ho!--my lord! my lady!

[Enter Lady Capulet.]

Lady Capulet

What noise is here?

Nurse

O lamentable day!

Lady Capulet

What is the matter?

Nurse

Look, look! O heavy day!

Lady Capulet

O me, O me!--my child, my only life! Revive, look up, or I will die with thee!-- Help, help!-- call help.

(Enter Capulet.)	[Enter Capulet.]
Capulet Be ashamed of yourself. Hurry up and bring Juliet!	**Capulet** For shame, bring Juliet forth; her lord is come.
Nurse She is dead. Deceased. Dead. Curse the day!	**Nurse** She's dead, deceas'd, she's dead; alack the day!
Lady Capulet Curse the day. She is dead! She is dead!	**Lady Capulet** Alack the day, she's dead, she's dead, she's dead!
Capulet Ha! Let me see her. She's cold. Her heart has stopped and her body is stiff. She has been dead for some time now. She is as dead as the sweetest flower in a field of frost. Cursed time! I am an unfortunate man!	**Capulet** Ha! let me see her:--out alas! she's cold; Her blood is settled, and her joints are stiff; Life and these lips have long been separated: Death lies on her like an untimely frost Upon the sweetest flower of all the field. Accursed time! unfortunate old man!
Nurse Oh, what a sad day!	**Nurse** O lamentable day!
Lady Capulet Oh, what a dreadful day!	**Lady Capulet** O woful time!
Capulet I am speechless.	**Capulet** Death, that hath ta'en her hence to make me wail, Ties up my tongue and will not let me speak.
(Enter Friar Lawrence and Paris, with Musicians.)	[Enter Friar Lawrence and Paris, with Musicians.]
Friar Lawrence Hey, is the bride ready to go to the church?	**Friar** Come, is the bride ready to go to church?
Capulet She is ready to go, but she will not be returning. Oh my son, the night before your wedding day, your bride has died. There she is. Death, who stole her innocence, is my son-in-law now.	**Capulet** Ready to go, but never to return:-- O son, the night before thy wedding day Hath death lain with thy bride:--there she lies, Flower as she was, deflowered by him. Death is my son-in-

Death is my heir. I believe I will die. Death is all there is left.

Paris
I have waited so long for this day and this is what I get.

Lady Capulet
Curse this awful, dreadful day! This is the most miserable hour time I ever saw. My one and only child, the one thing I had to rejoice, and death has taken her from me.

Nurse
Oh, terrible, terrible day! The saddest day! The most painful day, I have ever lived. Oh, hateful day! I have never seen a blacker day than this. Oh, painful day!

Paris
Tricked, divorced, wronged, spited, now dead! Death has stolen my love. Oh, love of my life! My love is dead!

Capulet
Despised, distressed, hated, martyred, killed! What a terrible time! Why now? Why does my only child have to die? My child! Oh, child! Take my soul and not my child's. My child is dead and so is my joy.

Friar Lawrence
Be at peace, now. What a shame! But, we can't solve anything with all of this confusion. She was a gift from heaven, and now to heaven, she has returned. She is better off. She has eternal life. All you wanted was for her to be married. That was your idea of heaven, but you

law, death is my heir; My daughter he hath wedded: I will die. And leave him all; life, living, all is death's.

Paris
Have I thought long to see this morning's face, And doth it give me such a sight as this?

Lady Capulet
Accurs'd, unhappy, wretched, hateful day! Most miserable hour that e'er time saw In lasting labour of his pilgrimage! But one, poor one, one poor and loving child, But one thing to rejoice and solace in, And cruel death hath catch'd it from my sight!

Nurse
O woe! O woeful, woeful, woeful day! Most lamentable day, most woeful day That ever, ever, I did yet behold! O day! O day! O day! O hateful day! Never was seen so black a day as this: O woeful day! O woeful day!

Paris
Beguil'd, divorced, wronged, spited, slain! Most detestable death, by thee beguil'd, By cruel cruel thee quite overthrown!-- O love! O life!-- not life, but love in death!

Capulet
Despis'd, distressed, hated, martyr'd, kill'd!-- Uncomfortable time, why cam'st thou now To murder, murder our solemnity?-- O child! O child!--my soul, and not my child!-- Dead art thou, dead!--alack, my child is dead; And with my child my joys are buried!

Friar
Peace, ho, for shame! confusion's cure lives not In these confusions. Heaven and yourself Had part in this fair maid; now heaven hath all, And all the better is it for the maid: Your part in her you could not keep from death; But heaven keeps his part in eternal life. The most you

cry because she has inherited the true heaven. Your love for her makes you crazy. It is better to die young. Dry up your tears and bring your best rosemary to place on her corpse. Take her to the church in her best clothes as the customs demand. Although we are sad, we should be happy for her.

Capulet
Everything we prepared for the celebration is now for a funeral. Change the happy music to sad, the wedding food to a burial feast, and the bridal flowers to a funeral spray. Just reverse everything.

Friar Lawrence
Go everyone. Let's get prepared for her funeral. Let's not stand in the way of God's will.

(Exit Capulet, Lady Capulet, Paris, and Friar.)

First Musician
Well, we may put up our instruments and leave.

Nurse
Yes, good men. Go ahead and pack up. This is a pitiful day.

(Exit Nurse.)

First Musician
I think things could get better.

---

sought was her promotion; For 'twas your heaven she should be advanc'd: And weep ye now, seeing she is advanc'd Above the clouds, as high as heaven itself? O, in this love, you love your child so ill That you run mad, seeing that she is well: She's not well married that lives married long: But she's best married that dies married young. Dry up your tears, and stick your rosemary On this fair corse; and, as the custom is, In all her best array bear her to church; For though fond nature bids us all lament, Yet nature's tears are reason's merriment.

Capulet
All things that we ordained festival Turn from their office to black funeral: Our instruments to melancholy bells; Our wedding cheer to a sad burial feast; Our solemn hymns to sullen dirges change; Our bridal flowers serve for a buried corse, And all things change them to the contrary.

Friar
Sir, go you in,--and, madam, go with him;-- And go, Sir Paris;--every one prepare To follow this fair corse unto her grave: The heavens do lower upon you for some ill; Move them no more by crossing their high will.

[Exeunt Capulet, Lady Capulet, Paris, and Friar.]

1 Musician
Faith, we may put up our pipes and be gone.

Nurse
Honest good fellows, ah, put up, put up; For well you know this is a pitiful case.

[Exit.]

1 Musician
Ay, by my troth, the case may be amended.

(Enter Peter.)	[Enter Peter.]
Peter	**Peter**
Musicians, play "Heart's Ease." If you want me to live, play "Heart's Ease."	Musicians, O, musicians, 'Heart's ease,' 'Heart's ease': O, an you will have me live, play 'Heart's ease.'
First Musician	**1 Musician**
Why "Heart's Ease?"	Why 'Heart's ease'?
Peter	**Peter**
Because, my heart is filled with sadness. Oh, play me some comforting song.	O, musicians, because my heart itself plays 'My heart is full of woe': O, play me some merry dump to comfort me.
First Musician	**1 Musician**
This is not the right time to play music.	Not a dump we: 'tis no time to play now.
Peter	**Peter**
You will not play?	You will not then?
First Musician	**1 Musician**
No.	No.
Peter	**Peter**
Then, you're gonna get it.	I will then give it you soundly.
First Musician	**1 Musician**
Get what?	What will you give us?
Peter	**Peter**
You'll get no money, I swear! You minstrel!	No money, on my faith; but the gleek,--I will give you the minstrel.
First Musician	**1 Musician**
You are nothing but a servant.	Then will I give you the serving-creature.
Peter	**Peter**
Then, I will serve up a dagger for you. I will make you sing do-re-mi. Do you hear me?	Then will I lay the serving-creature's dagger on your pate. I will carry no crotchets: I'll re you, I'll fa you: do you note me?
First Musician	**1 Musician**

You can't make us sing!

Second Musician
Please, put away your dagger and stop messing around.

Peter
You don't like my joking around? I will beat you with my jokes. Answer me this: Doesn't music soothe the soul like the song says, "When grief wounds your heart and sadness grips your mind, listen to the silver sound of music."
What do you say to that?

First Musician
Because the sound of silver is a happy sound.

Peter
(To the second Musician.) What do you say, sir?

Second Musician
I think it's because musicians will play for silver.

Peter
That's a good answer. (To the third Musician.) What do you think?

Third Musician
I have no idea.

Peter
Well, I'll tell you. You're the singer, for heaven's sake. If it were not for music, you would have no songs to sing. "Music with her silver sound makes you feel fine."

(Exit Peter.)

An you re us and fa us, you note us.

2 Musician
Pray you put up your dagger, and put out your wit.

Peter
Then have at you with my wit! I will dry-beat you with an iron wit, and put up my iron dagger.--Answer me like men:

'When griping grief the heart doth wound, And doleful dumps the mind oppress, Then music with her silver sound'--

why 'silver sound'? why 'music with her silver sound'?-- What say you, Simon Catling?

1 Musician
Marry, sir, because silver hath a sweet sound.

Peter
Pretty!--What say you, Hugh Rebeck?

2 Musician
I say 'silver sound' because musicians sound for silver.

Peter
Pretty too!--What say you, James Soundpost?

3 Musician
Faith, I know not what to say.

Peter
O, I cry you mercy; you are the singer: I will say for you. It is 'music with her silver sound' because musicians have no gold for sounding:--

'Then music with her silver sound With speedy help doth lend redress.'

	[Exit.]
First Musician What a crazy man!	**1 Musician** What a pestilent knave is this same!
Second Musician Don't worry about him. Come on. We'll wait for the mourners and stay for dinner.	**2 Musician** Hang him, Jack!--Come, we'll in here; tarry for the mourners, and stay dinner.
(Exit all.)	[Exeunt.]

Act V

Scene I: A street in Mantua.

(Enter Romeo.)

Romeo
If my dreams are correct, I am going to hear some good news today. My heart is light, and I feel cheerful today. I dreamed my lady came and found me dead. She revived me with her kisses. Then, I became an emperor. Oh, how wonderful it would be to have my love with me, when just thinking about her fills me with joy.

(Enter Balthasar.)

Hey Balthasar! How are you? Any news from Verona? Did you bring me letters from the friar? How is my lady? Is my father okay? How is Juliet? Nothing can be wrong, if she is well.

Balthasar
She is well and nothing is wrong, except her body is in Capulet's tomb. She is with the angels. I saw her laid to rest in her family's vault. So, I came to tell you. I'm sorry to have to tell you such bad news, but I thought you'd want to know.

Romeo
Are you sure? Then, I curse the stars. Get me some ink and paper, and hire some horses. I will leave here tonight.

Balthasar
Please, sir, think it through. You are not

Romeo
If I may trust the flattering eye of sleep, My dreams presage some joyful news at hand; My bosom's lord sits lightly in his throne; And all this day an unaccustom'd spirit Lifts me above the ground with cheerful thoughts. I dreamt my lady came and found me dead,-- Strange dream, that gives a dead man leave to think!-- And breath'd such life with kisses in my lips, That I reviv'd, and was an emperor. Ah me! how sweet is love itself possess'd, When but love's shadows are so rich in joy!

[Enter Balthasar.]

 News from Verona!--How now, Balthasar? Dost thou not bring me letters from the friar? How doth my lady? Is my father well? How fares my Juliet? that I ask again; For nothing can be ill if she be well.

Balthasar
Then she is well, and nothing can be ill: Her body sleeps in Capel's monument, And her immortal part with angels lives. I saw her laid low in her kindred's vault, And presently took post to tell it you: O, pardon me for bringing these ill news, Since you did leave it for my office, sir.

Romeo
Is it even so? then I defy you, stars!-- Thou know'st my lodging: get me ink and paper, And hire post-horses. I will hence to-night.

Balthasar
I do beseech you, sir, have patience: Your looks

thinking clearly. You are going to get into trouble.

Romeo
Don't worry about me. Just go get the things I need. Do you have any letters from the friar?

Balthasar
No, my lord.

Romeo
It doesn't matter, anyway. Go on and get the horses. I'll be with you in a minute.

(Exit Balthasar.)

Well, Juliet. I will be with you tonight. Now, how will I do it? I remember an apothecary who lives around here who could give me a poisonous tonic. He looked worn out with his shabby clothes and thin body. I remember the crazy things in his shop, and thinking if ever I needed a poison to take my life, this is where I would come. I need him now. This is his house, but he is closed. Hello, pharmacist!

(Enter apothecary.)

Apothecary
Who is calling me so loudly?

are pale and wild, and do import Some misadventure.

Romeo
Tush, thou art deceiv'd: Leave me, and do the thing I bid thee do. Hast thou no letters to me from the friar?

Balthasar
No, my good lord.

Romeo
No matter: get thee gone, And hire those horses; I'll be with thee straight.

[Exit Balthasar.]

Well, Juliet, I will lie with thee to-night. Let's see for means;--O mischief, thou art swift To enter in the thoughts of desperate men! I do remember an apothecary,-- And hereabouts he dwells,--which late I noted In tatter'd weeds, with overwhelming brows, Culling of simples; meagre were his looks, Sharp misery had worn him to the bones; And in his needy shop a tortoise hung, An alligator stuff'd, and other skins Of ill-shaped fishes; and about his shelves A beggarly account of empty boxes, Green earthen pots, bladders, and musty seeds, Remnants of packthread, and old cakes of roses, Were thinly scatter'd, to make up a show. Noting this penury, to myself I said, An if a man did need a poison now, Whose sale is present death in Mantua, Here lives a caitiff wretch would sell it him. O, this same thought did but forerun my need; And this same needy man must sell it me. As I remember, this should be the house: Being holiday, the beggar's shop is shut.-- What, ho! apothecary!

[Enter Apothecary.]

Apothecary
Who calls so loud?

Romeo
Come here, man. I see that you are poor, and I have money for a bit of poison that will work quickly and is strong enough to kill a man.

Apothecary
I have some, but Mantuan laws forbid the selling of it.

Romeo
How do you fear death when you are already poor and wretched? Your cheeks are sunken in with famine and your eyes show signs of starvation. You look like a beggar. The world is not your friend, nor the law. The world will not help you become rich. It aims to keep you poor. But, if you break the law, you may have this money.

Apothecary
Not I, but my poverty, consents.

Romeo
Then, I pay your poverty.

Apothecary
Here, put this in any liquid and drink it. When you drink it all, even if you had the strength of twenty men, you will die.

Romeo
Here is your gold, the killer of more men than this poison. It is more poisonous than what you have given me. Farewell, and buy some food to put some meat on your bones. Come on sweet drink, go with me to Juliet's grave, where I will use you.

Romeo
Come hither, man.--I see that thou art poor; Hold, there is forty ducats: let me have A dram of poison; such soon-speeding gear As will disperse itself through all the veins That the life-weary taker mall fall dead; And that the trunk may be discharg'd of breath As violently as hasty powder fir'd Doth hurry from the fatal cannon's womb.

Apothecary
Such mortal drugs I have; but Mantua's law Is death to any he that utters them.

Romeo
Art thou so bare and full of wretchedness And fear'st to die? famine is in thy cheeks, Need and oppression starveth in thine eyes, Contempt and beggary hangs upon thy back, The world is not thy friend, nor the world's law: The world affords no law to make thee rich; Then be not poor, but break it and take this.

Apothecary
My poverty, but not my will consents.

Romeo
I pay thy poverty, and not thy will.

Apothecary
Put this in any liquid thing you will, And drink it off; and, if you had the strength Of twenty men, it would despatch you straight.

Romeo
There is thy gold; worse poison to men's souls, Doing more murders in this loathsome world Than these poor compounds that thou mayst not sell: I sell thee poison; thou hast sold me none. Farewell: buy food and get thyself in flesh.-- Come, cordial and not poison, go with me To Juliet's grave; for there must I use thee.

(Exit all.)	[Exeunt.]

Scene II: Friar Lawrence's cell.

(Enter Friar John.)

Friar John Holy Franciscan Friar! Hello, brother!	**Friar John** Holy Franciscan friar! brother, ho!
(Enter Friar Lawrence.)	[Enter Friar Lawrence.]
Friar Lawrence Is that the voice of Friar John of Mantua? Welcome. How is Romeo? Do you have a letter from him?	**Friar Lawrence** This same should be the voice of Friar John. Welcome from Mantua: what says Romeo? Or, if his mind be writ, give me his letter.
Friar John I don't know. I have been here visiting the sick. We were all put into isolation because of the fear of contagion. So, I haven't been to Mantua.	**Friar John** Going to find a barefoot brother out, One of our order, to associate me, Here in this city visiting the sick, And finding him, the searchers of the town, Suspecting that we both were in a house Where the infectious pestilence did reign, Seal'd up the doors, and would not let us forth; So that my speed to Mantua there was stay'd.
Friar Lawrence Who took my letters, then?	**Friar Lawrence** Who bare my letter, then, to Romeo?
Friar John No one. I still have it. I could not even get a messenger because of the fear of infection.	**Friar John** I could not send it,--here it is again,-- Nor get a messenger to bring it thee, So fearful were they of infection.
Friar Lawrence Oh, no! If Romeo did not get the letter, then I fear he is in danger. Friar John, go now and get me a crowbar. Bring it back here, quickly.	**Friar Lawrence** Unhappy fortune! by my brotherhood, The letter was not nice, but full of charge Of dear import; and the neglecting it May do much danger. Friar John, go hence; Get me an iron crow and bring it straight Unto my cell.
Friar John Okay, I'll go as fast as I can.	**Friar John** Brother, I'll go and bring it thee.

(Exit Friar John.)	[Exit.]
Friar Lawrence Now, I must go to the tomb alone. Juliet will be awake in three hours. She will hate me if Romeo is not there. But, I will write to Romeo again and keep her in my cell until he gets here. Poor living soul, closed up in a dead man's tomb!	**Friar Lawrence** Now must I to the monument alone; Within this three hours will fair Juliet wake: She will beshrew me much that Romeo Hath had no notice of these accidents; But I will write again to Mantua, And keep her at my cell till Romeo come;-- Poor living corse, clos'd in a dead man's tomb!
(Exit.)	[Exit.]

Scene III: A churchyard with the tomb of the Capulets.

(Enter Paris and his Page, bearing flowers and a torch.)

Paris

Give me the torch, boy, and stand back. Better yet, put it out. I don't want to be seen out here. Go over by that tree and put your ear to the ground. If you hear someone coming, whistle a warning. Give me those flowers and do as I say.

Page

(To himself.) Okay, but I am afraid to stand alone in the graveyard.

(Retires.)

Paris

Oh, my sweet flower. I bring you flowers for thy bridal bed. Your canopy is dust and stones. I will water them with my tears. I promise to come every night and bring flowers and weep.

(The Page whistles.)

I hear the boy's warning. Someone is coming and keeping me from mourning my love. Someone with a torch! I must hide in the darkness.

(Retires.)

(Enter Romeo and Balthasar with a torch and tools.)

Paris

Give me thy torch, boy: hence, and stand aloof;-- Yet put it out, for I would not be seen. Under yond yew tree lay thee all along, Holding thine ear close to the hollow ground; So shall no foot upon the churchyard tread,-- Being loose, unfirm, with digging up of graves,-- But thou shalt hear it: whistle then to me, As signal that thou hear'st something approach. Give me those flowers. Do as I bid thee, go.

Page

[Aside.] I am almost afraid to stand alone Here in the churchyard; yet I will adventure.

[Retires.]

Paris

Sweet flower, with flowers thy bridal bed I strew: O woe! thy canopy is dust and stones! Which with sweet water nightly I will dew; Or, wanting that, with tears distill'd by moans: The obsequies that I for thee will keep, Nightly shall be to strew thy grave and weep.

[The Page whistles.]

The boy gives warning something doth approach. What cursed foot wanders this way to-night, To cross my obsequies and true love's rite? What, with a torch! muffle me, night, awhile.

[Retires.]

[Enter Romeo and Balthasar with a torch, mattock, &c.]

Romeo
Give me the axe and the crowbar. Here, take this letter, and deliver it to my father in the morning. Give me the torch, and promise me that no matter what you hear or see, you will not interfere. I am going in there partly to see my love's face one more time, and to get a ring from her finger that I must use. So, go on, but if you come back I will tear you limb from limb and spread you about this graveyard. I am as wild and fierce as a tiger!

Balthasar
I'll go, sir, and not bother you.

Romeo
Good friend, take this and live prosperously. Farewell, good fellow.

Balthasar
(To himself.) I'll hide here, because I am afraid he is up to no good.

(Retires.)

Romeo
Damned tomb, house of death, filled with the dearest that ever tread the earth, I will open your rotten jaws…

(Opens the door.)

…and fill you with more food.

Paris

Romeo
Give me that mattock and the wrenching iron. Hold, take this letter; early in the morning See thou deliver it to my lord and father. Give me the light; upon thy life I charge thee, Whate'er thou hear'st or seest, stand all aloof And do not interrupt me in my course. Why I descend into this bed of death Is partly to behold my lady's face, But chiefly to take thence from her dead finger A precious ring,--a ring that I must use In dear employment: therefore hence, be gone:-- But if thou, jealous, dost return to pry In what I further shall intend to do, By heaven, I will tear thee joint by joint, And strew this hungry churchyard with thy limbs: The time and my intents are savage-wild; More fierce and more inexorable far Than empty tigers or the roaring sea.

Balthasar
I will be gone, sir, and not trouble you.

Romeo
So shalt thou show me friendship.--Take thou that: Live, and be prosperous: and farewell, good fellow.

Balthasar
For all this same, I'll hide me hereabout: His looks I fear, and his intents I doubt.

[Retires.]

Romeo
Thou detestable maw, thou womb of death, Gorg'd with the dearest morsel of the earth, Thus I enforce thy rotten jaws to open,

[Breaking open the door of the monument.]

And, in despite, I'll cram thee with more food!

Paris

That is the Montague who murdered my love's cousin and caused my bride to die from grief. He has come to do something awful to the dead bodies. I will capture him.

(Advances.)

Stop villainous Montague! How can you seek revenge on the dead? I arrest you. Obey me and come because you are going to die.

Romeo
That is why I'm here. I am a desperate man. Don't tempt me. Go away and leave me alone. I beg you, young man, do not make me kill you. I am here to kill myself, not you. Go away and let a madman finish himself.

Paris
No, I will not let you. I arrest you as a felon.

Romeo
Let's go then, boy.

(They fight.)

Page
Oh, lord. They are fighting. I will go call the police.

(Exit Page.)

Paris
You have stabbed me. (Falls.) Please be merciful and put me with Juliet.

This is that banish'd haughty Montague That murder'd my love's cousin,--with which grief, It is supposed, the fair creature died,-- And here is come to do some villanous shame To the dead bodies: I will apprehend him.--

[Advances.]

Stop thy unhallow'd toil, vile Montague! Can vengeance be pursu'd further than death? Condemned villain, I do apprehend thee; Obey, and go with me; for thou must die.

Romeo
I must indeed; and therefore came I hither.-- Good gentle youth, tempt not a desperate man; Fly hence and leave me:--think upon these gone; Let them affright thee.--I beseech thee, youth, Put not another sin upon my head By urging me to fury: O, be gone! By heaven, I love thee better than myself; For I come hither arm'd against myself: Stay not, be gone;--live, and hereafter say, A madman's mercy bid thee run away.

Paris
I do defy thy conjurations, And apprehend thee for a felon here.

Romeo
Wilt thou provoke me? then have at thee, boy!

[They fight.]

Page
O lord, they fight! I will go call the watch.

[Exit.]

Paris
O, I am slain! [Falls.] If thou be merciful, Open the tomb, lay me with Juliet.

(Dies.)

Romeo

Let me look at you. You are Mercutio's relative, Paris. Wasn't it my man who said that you were going to marry Juliet? Or did I dream that? Am I going mad? Join me in my misfortune, Paris, and I will bury you in a triumphant grave. This does not look like a grave, with the light from Juliet's beautiful face inside. Here, this is where dead men lay.

(Lays Paris in the tomb.)

How is it that men feel happiness when they are about to die? Is it enlightenment? I will call this enlightenment. Oh, my love! My wife! Death that took away your breath did not have the power to take away your beauty. You are not conquered. You still have color in your cheeks and lips. Tybalt, lying over there in your bloody sheet, I do you a favor by taking the hand that killed you and kill myself. Forgive me, cousin! Ah, Juliet, why are you still so beautiful? Is death so jealous that he has brought you here to be his lover? I will not leave you in this dark place for him. I will stay with you and the worms that are your servants. Here, I will set up my everlasting rest and shake the yoke of this world. Eyes, take your last look! Arms, take your last embrace, and lips, the doors of breath take your last kiss. Come bitter death, I will not bargain with you. Here's to my love! (Drinks.) The drugs work quickly, so with a kiss I die.

(Dies.)

(Enter, at the other end of the Churchyard, Friar Lawrence with a lantern, crowbar and shovel.)

[Dies.]

Romeo

In faith, I will.--Let me peruse this face:-- Mercutio's kinsman, noble County Paris!-- What said my man, when my betossed soul Did not attend him as we rode? I think He told me Paris should have married Juliet: Said he not so? or did I dream it so? Or am I mad, hearing him talk of Juliet, To think it was so?--O, give me thy hand, One writ with me in sour misfortune's book! I'll bury thee in a triumphant grave;-- A grave? O, no, a lanthorn, slaught'red youth, For here lies Juliet, and her beauty makes This vault a feasting presence full of light. Death, lie thou there, by a dead man interr'd.

[Laying Paris in the monument.]

How oft when men are at the point of death Have they been merry! which their keepers call A lightning before death: O, how may I Call this a lightning?--O my love! my wife! Death, that hath suck'd the honey of thy breath, Hath had no power yet upon thy beauty: Thou art not conquer'd; beauty's ensign yet Is crimson in thy lips and in thy cheeks, And death's pale flag is not advanced there.-- Tybalt, liest thou there in thy bloody sheet? O, what more favour can I do to thee Than with that hand that cut thy youth in twain To sunder his that was thine enemy? Forgive me, cousin!--Ah, dear Juliet, Why art thou yet so fair? Shall I believe That unsubstantial death is amorous; And that the lean abhorred monster keeps Thee here in dark to be his paramour? For fear of that I still will stay with thee, And never from this palace of dim night Depart again: here, here will I remain With worms that are thy chambermaids: O, here Will I set up my everlasting rest; And shake the yoke of inauspicious stars From this world-wearied flesh.--Eyes, look your last! Arms, take your last embrace! and, lips, O you The doors of breath, seal with a righteous kiss A dateless

Friar Lawrence
Saint Francis, give me speed! I have stepped over so many graves tonight. Who's there? Who is it in this place so late? Is it the dead?

Balthasar
It is your friend.

Friar Lawrence
Oh, good. Tell me, friend, what light is that over there by the Capulet's tomb?

Balthasar
It is my master, the one you love so much.

Friar Lawrence
Who is it?

Balthasar
Romeo.

Friar Lawrence
How long has he been in there?

Balthasar
About a half an hour.

Friar Lawrence

---

bargain to engrossing death!-- Come, bitter conduct, come, unsavoury guide! Thou desperate pilot, now at once run on The dashing rocks thy sea-sick weary bark! Here's to my love! [Drinks.]--O true apothecary! Thy drugs are quick.--Thus with a kiss I die.

[Dies.]

[Enter, at the other end of the Churchyard, Friar Lawrence, with a lantern, crow, and spade.]

Friar
Saint Francis be my speed! how oft to-night Have my old feet stumbled at graves!--Who's there? Who is it that consorts, so late, the dead?

Balthasar
Here's one, a friend, and one that knows you well.

Friar
Bliss be upon you! Tell me, good my friend, What torch is yond that vainly lends his light To grubs and eyeless skulls? as I discern, It burneth in the Capels' monument.

Balthasar
It doth so, holy sir; and there's my master, One that you love.

Friar
Who is it?

Balthasar
Romeo.

Friar
How long hath he been there?

Balthasar
Full half an hour.

Friar

Go with me.

Balthasar
No. My master thinks I am gone and threatened me with death if I interrupted him.

Friar Lawrence
Stay then. I'll go alone, although fear grips me.

Balthasar
I fell asleep under this tree and dreamed that my master was fighting someone, and that he killed him.

Friar Lawrence
Romeo! (Goes forward.) Oh, no, what is this blood stain? What do these bloody swords mean?

(Enters the tomb.)

Romeo! You are so pale! And, Paris, too? What a terrible time! The lady stirs.

(Juliet wakes and stirs.)

Juliet
Oh, Friar, where is my lord? I remember where I am supposed to be, but where is Romeo?

(Noise from within.)

Friar Lawrence
I hear some noise. Come on, Juliet. Our plan is all messed up. Your husband is dead, so is Pairs. I'll hide you in a convent with some nuns. Hurry, someone is coming. Let's go.

Go with me to the vault.

Balthasar
I dare not, sir; My master knows not but I am gone hence; And fearfully did menace me with death If I did stay to look on his intents.

Friar
Stay then; I'll go alone:--fear comes upon me;
O, much I fear some ill unlucky thing.

Balthasar
As I did sleep under this yew tree here, I dreamt my master and another fought, And that my master slew him.

Friar
Romeo! [Advances.] Alack, alack! what blood is this which stains The stony entrance of this sepulchre?-- What mean these masterless and gory swords To lie discolour'd by this place of peace?

[Enters the monument.]

Romeo! O, pale!--Who else? what, Paris too? And steep'd in blood?--Ah, what an unkind hour Is guilty of this lamentable chance!--The lady stirs.

[Juliet wakes and stirs.]

Juliet
O comfortable friar! where is my lord?-- I do remember well where I should be, And there I am:--where is my Romeo?

[Noise within.]

Friar
I hear some noise.--Lady, come from that nest Of death, contagion, and unnatural sleep: A greater power than we can contradict Hath thwarted our intents:--come, come away! Thy

(Noise from within.) I can't stay any longer.

Juliet
Go, then. I'm not leaving.

(Exit Friar Lawrence.)

What's this? My true love has a cup in his hand. Poisonous drink, I think has taken his life. There is none left for me. I will kiss your lips and pray some poison remains to help me die.

(Kisses him.)

First Watch
Lead the way, boy.

Juliet
I hear another noise. I must hurry. Oh good, Romeo's dagger!

(Snatching Romeo's dagger.)

This is the place where knives go. (Stabs herself.) Now, let me die.

(Falls on Romeo's body and dies.)

(Enter Watch, with the Paris's Page.)

Page
This is the place. See the burning torch.

First Watch
The ground is bloody. Search the churchyard.

husband in thy bosom there lies dead; And Paris too:--come, I'll dispose of thee Among a sisterhood of holy nuns: Stay not to question, for the watch is coming. Come, go, good Juliet [noise within],--I dare no longer stay.

Juliet
Go, get thee hence, for I will not away.--

[Exit Friar Lawrence.]

What's here? a cup, clos'd in my true love's hand? Poison, I see, hath been his timeless end:-- O churl! drink all, and left no friendly drop To help me after?--I will kiss thy lips; Haply some poison yet doth hang on them, To make me die with a restorative.

[Kisses him.]

Thy lips are warm!

1 Watch
[Within.] Lead, boy:--which way?

Juliet
Yea, noise?--Then I'll be brief.--O happy dagger!

[Snatching Romeo's dagger.]

This is thy sheath [stabs herself]; there rest, and let me die.

[Falls on Romeo's body and dies.]

[Enter Watch, with the Page of Paris.]

Page
This is the place; there, where the torch doth burn.

1 Watch
The ground is bloody; search about the

Go and if you find someone attack.

(Exit some of the Watch.)

What a pitiful sight! Here is the count, murdered. Here is Juliet, bleeding, but she was supposed to be dead. She was buried two days ago. Go tell the Prince. Run to the Capulets and get the Montagues.

(Exit others of the Watch.)

We are in the sight of some terrible, unexplainable happenings.

(Enter some of the watch with Balthasar.)

Second Watch
Here's Romeo's man. We found him in the churchyard.

First Watch
Hold him until the Prince gets here.

(Enter others of the Watch with Friar Lawrence.)

Third Watch
Here is a friar, trembling and weeping. We took this axe and shovel from him. He was coming from the graveyard.

First Watch
That is very odd. We better keep him, too.

(Enter the Prince and Attendants.)

Prince
What is going on that you feel the need to wake us up so early?

(Enter Capulet, Lady Capulet, and others.)

---

churchyard: Go, some of you, whoe'er you find attach.

[Exeunt some of the Watch.]

Pitiful sight! here lies the county slain;-- And Juliet bleeding; warm, and newly dead, Who here hath lain this two days buried.-- Go, tell the prince;--run to the Capulets,-- Raise up the Montagues,--some others search:--

[Exeunt others of the Watch.]

We see the ground whereon these woes do lie; But the true ground of all these piteous woes We cannot without circumstance descry.

[Re-enter some of the Watch with Balthasar.]

2 Watch
Here's Romeo's man; we found him in the churchyard.

1 Watch
Hold him in safety till the prince come hither.

[Re-enter others of the Watch with Friar Lawrence.]

3 Watch
Here is a friar, that trembles, sighs, and weeps: We took this mattock and this spade from him As he was coming from this churchyard side.

1 Watch
A great suspicion: stay the friar too.

[Enter the Prince and Attendants.]

Prince
What misadventure is so early up, That calls our person from our morning's rest?

[Enter Capulet, Lady Capulet, and others.]

Capulet
What is the problem? Why are they crying out?

Lady Capulet
People in the street cry Romeo, and some cry Juliet. Some are crying Paris, and all of them are running towards our monument.

Prince
What is everyone crying about?

First Watch
Sir, here lies the body of Count Paris. He has been murdered. Romeo is dead, too. So is Juliet, although she was thought to be dead, appears to have just been killed.

Prince
Search and find out how these murders happened.

First Watch
Here is a friar with tools to open a tomb and Romeo's man.

Capulet
Oh, heaven! Oh, wife, look at our daughter's blood. The knife of the Montague is in our daughter's chest.

Lady Capulet
Oh me! The sight of all this death is like a bell reminding me that my time is coming soon.

(Enter Montague.)

Montague

Capulet
What should it be, that they so shriek abroad?

Lady Capulet
The people in the street cry Romeo, Some Juliet, and some Paris; and all run, With open outcry, toward our monument.

Prince
What fear is this which startles in our ears?

1 Watch
Sovereign, here lies the County Paris slain; And Romeo dead; and Juliet, dead before, Warm and new kill'd.

Prince
Search, seek, and know how this foul murder comes.

1 Watch
Here is a friar, and slaughter'd Romeo's man, With instruments upon them fit to open These dead men's tombs.

Capulet
O heaven!--O wife, look how our daughter bleeds! This dagger hath mista'en,--for, lo, his house Is empty on the back of Montague,-- And it mis-sheathed in my daughter's bosom!

Lady Capulet
O me! this sight of death is as a bell That warns my old age to a sepulchre.

[Enter Montague and others.]

Prince
Come, Montague; for thou art early up, To see thy son and heir more early down.

Montague

Sir, my wife died tonight. She died from grief because of my son's exile. What else must I endure?

Prince
Look and you will see.

Montague
Oh, you selfish boy. How could you not wait? Fathers are supposed to die before their sons.

Prince
Everyone be quiet and do not make any allegations until we know what happened and how it started. Then, I will let you express your pain. Meanwhile, let's be patient. Bring in the suspects.

Friar Lawrence
I am the greatest at fault, but I could do the least. I know you suspect me of murder, but I am not guilty, and I am not innocent.

Prince
Then tell us what you know.

Friar Lawrence
I will be brief, because I think I will not live long enough to tell a boring story. Romeo was Juliet's husband. And she was trying to be faithful to Romeo. I married them on the day Romeo killed Tybalt, which caused him to be exiled. So, Juliet wept for Romeo, and to keep her from killing herself I gave her a sleeping potion. The potion made her look dead. Then, I wrote to Romeo for him to come and claim her from the tomb when she awoke, but he never got my letter. So, I came to retrieve her and found Paris and Romeo, both dead. When she awoke I tried to get her to come with me, but

Alas, my liege, my wife is dead to-night; Grief of my son's exile hath stopp'd her breath: What further woe conspires against mine age?

Prince
Look, and thou shalt see.

Montague
O thou untaught! what manners is in this, To press before thy father to a grave?

Prince
Seal up the mouth of outrage for a while, Till we can clear these ambiguities, And know their spring, their head, their true descent; And then will I be general of your woes, And lead you even to death: meantime forbear, And let mischance be slave to patience.-- Bring forth the parties of suspicion.

Friar
I am the greatest, able to do least, Yet most suspected, as the time and place Doth make against me, of this direful murder; And here I stand, both to impeach and purge Myself condemned and myself excus'd.

Prince
Then say at once what thou dost know in this.

Friar
I will be brief, for my short date of breath Is not so long as is a tedious tale. Romeo, there dead, was husband to that Juliet; And she, there dead, that Romeo's faithful wife: I married them; and their stol'n marriage day Was Tybalt's doomsday, whose untimely death Banish'd the new-made bridegroom from this city; For whom, and not for Tybalt, Juliet pin'd. You, to remove that siege of grief from her, Betroth'd, and would have married her perforce, To County Paris:--then comes she to me, And with wild looks, bid me devise some means To rid her from this second marriage, Or in my cell

she would not leave. I got scared and left, but she stayed to take her own life. Her nurse knows the truth. If, this is my fault let me be sacrificed and held accountable under the severest penalty of the law.

Prince
We have always known you to be holy. Where's Romeo's man? What does he have to say about all of this?

Balthasar
I told Romeo the news of Juliet's death. Then, he came from Mantua to this place. He gave me this letter to give to his father and threatened me with death, if I did not leave. I just went over there by that tree.

Prince
Give me the letter. I will look at it. Where is the boy that got the Watch? Sir, why was your master here?

there would she kill herself. Then gave I her, so tutored by my art, A sleeping potion; which so took effect As I intended, for it wrought on her The form of death: meantime I writ to Romeo That he should hither come as this dire night, To help to take her from her borrow'd grave, Being the time the potion's force should cease. But he which bore my letter, Friar John, Was stay'd by accident; and yesternight Return'd my letter back. Then all alone At the prefixed hour of her waking Came I to take her from her kindred's vault; Meaning to keep her closely at my cell Till I conveniently could send to Romeo: But when I came,--some minute ere the time Of her awaking,--here untimely lay The noble Paris and true Romeo dead. She wakes; and I entreated her come forth And bear this work of heaven with patience: But then a noise did scare me from the tomb; And she, too desperate, would not go with me, But, as it seems, did violence on herself. All this I know; and to the marriage Her nurse is privy: and if ought in this Miscarried by my fault, let my old life Be sacrific'd, some hour before his time, Unto the rigour of severest law.

Prince
We still have known thee for a holy man.-- Where's Romeo's man? what can he say in this?

Balthasar
I brought my master news of Juliet's death; And then in post he came from Mantua To this same place, to this same monument. This letter he early bid me give his father; And threaten'd me with death, going in the vault, If I departed not, and left him there.

Prince
Give me the letter,--I will look on it.-- Where is the county's page that rais'd the watch?-- Sirrah, what made your master in this place?

Boy

He came with flowers to place on his lady's grave. He made me stay back. Then, someone came with a light and started to open the tomb. My master drew on him. So, I ran to get the Watch.

Prince

This letter confirms the Friar's story. It describes their love and the news of her death. He writes that he bought poison to come here to die and be with Juliet forever. Where are Capulet and Montague? See what happens to people who bear hatred towards one another. Since I did not do anything about it, I have lost loved ones, too.

Capulet

Oh, brother Montague, give me your hand. For my daughter and your son, I can ask you for nothing.

Montague

But, I can give you something. I will raise a statue for her in pure gold in remembrance of her goodness for all of Verona to see.

Capulet

Then, I will make a statue of Romeo to lie beside Juliet. They were poor sacrifices of our hatred.

Prince

This is a terrible way to finally have peace. Even the sun is too sad to show her face. Let's go talk more of these sad things. Some things will be pardoned and some will be punished, but there will never be a story as sad as that of Romeo and Juliet.

(Exit all.)

Boy

He came with flowers to strew his lady's grave; And bid me stand aloof, and so I did: Anon comes one with light to ope the tomb; And by-and-by my master drew on him; And then I ran away to call the watch.

Prince

This letter doth make good the friar's words, Their course of love, the tidings of her death: And here he writes that he did buy a poison Of a poor 'pothecary, and therewithal Came to this vault to die, and lie with Juliet.-- Where be these enemies?--Capulet,--Montague,-- See what a scourge is laid upon your hate, That heaven finds means to kill your joys with love! And I, for winking at your discords too, Have lost a brace of kinsmen:--all are punish'd.

Capulet

O brother Montague, give me thy hand: This is my daughter's jointure, for no more Can I demand.

Montague

But I can give thee more: For I will raise her statue in pure gold; That while Verona by that name is known, There shall no figure at such rate be set As that of true and faithful Juliet.

Capulet

As rich shall Romeo's by his lady's lie; Poor sacrifices of our enmity!

Prince

A glooming peace this morning with it brings; The sun for sorrow will not show his head. Go hence, to have more talk of these sad things; Some shall be pardon'd, and some punished; For never was a story of more woe Than this of Juliet and her Romeo.

[Exeunt.]

| **The End** | **The End** |

Made in the USA
San Bernardino, CA
01 February 2017